THE DOOR BEFORE

By N. D. Wilson

Leepike Ridge
Boys of Blur

100 Cupboards Series

The Door Before (100 Cupboards Prequel)
100 Cupboards
Dandelion Fire
The Chestnut King

Ashtown Burials Series

The Dragon's Tooth
The Drowned Vault
Empire of Bones

THE DOOR BEFORE

PREQUEL TO THE 100 CUPBOARDS SERIES

Peachtree

N. D. Wilson

Random House 🏠 New York

Text copyright © 2017 by N. D. Wilson
Jacket art copyright © 2017 by Jakob Eirich

All rights reserved. Published in the United States by
Random House Children's Books, a division of
Penguin Random House LLC, New York.

Random House and the colophon are registered trademarks of
Penguin Random House LLC.

Visit us on the Web! randomhousekids.com

Educators and librarians, for a variety of teaching tools,
visit us at RHTeachersLibrarians.com

Library of Congress Cataloging-in-Publication Data
Names: Wilson, Nathan D., author
Title: The door before / N. D. Wilson.
Description: First edition. | New York : Random House, [2017] | Prequel to the 100
cupboards series. | Summary: When Hyacinth Smith moves with her family to a new
house, she discovers new friends and powerful enemies, and that her power with trees
opens ways between worlds.
Identifiers: LCCN 2016017403 | ISBN 978-0-449-81677-6 (hardback) |
ISBN 978-0-449-81678-3 (lib. bdg.) | ISBN 978-0-449-81679-0 (ebook)
Subjects: | CYAC: Magic—Fiction. | Space and time—Fiction. | Doors—Fiction.
| Trees—Fiction. | Witches—Fiction. | BISAC: JUVENILE FICTION / Action &
Adventure / General. | JUVENILE FICTION / Legends, Myths, Fables / General. |
JUVENILE FICTION / Boys & Men.
Classification: LCC PZ7.W69744 Do 2017 | DDC [Fic]—dc23

Printed in the United States of America
10 9 8 7 6 5 4 3 2 1
First Edition

For Bekah & Rachel,
We three, we happy three,
we band of brother and two sisters . . .

Trees keep time the way time is meant to be kept.
They wrap the years around themselves in ringed layers,
expanding as the ages do. And when time forks,
so do the trees, stretching branches into cousin futures,
plunging roots into sister pasts, binding
every leaf into the one story, the only story.
The story that began. The story that cannot end,
because it can never stop growing.

ONE

EVERY STORM WILL SPILL a final drop. Every mortal will draw a final breath. Every road will carry a final traveler.

High on a towering cliff of sandstone, above a gray churning sea and below swaying groves of redwood trees, all three of those finales were coming to pass in the same place and in the same dusky twilight.

While hungry waves watched, a coal-colored truck with only one headlight crawled along the cliff's lip, tugging a stubby silver camper behind it, windows gleaming wet.

For more than a century, the crude cliff road had carried its travelers safely through gullies and over rises, well back from where the continent ended and the Pacific Ocean began. But there is nothing in the world so greedy and determined as the sea. Meadows of wildflowers and stands of cedars had all been chewed away, leaving nothing to border the road but air and floating gulls and drifting spray from the largest waves.

1

The road's final traveler was a twelve-year-old girl in the camper trailer, seated on a defeated old cushion on a little bench in the very back, beside a fold-up table covered with loose playing cards. She was Hyacinth Maxine Smith, and her eyes were on the western horizon, where the faint white glow of the sun was just vanishing. Her left hand propped up her chin, and her right was rubbing her little brother Lawrence's blond buzzed head as he snoozed in her lap.

Hyacinth was the final traveler only because her four siblings were farther forward in the trailer, even if only slightly. Daniel was in a flannel sleeping bag, snoring on the narrow slice of floor. His wide, angular, sixteen-year-old shoulders had grown wider and more angular in recent months. His hair was darker and even shorter than Lawrence's. Harriet was humming on the trailer's fraying sofa with her legs curled beneath her. She was fourteen, her sunny brown hair was always in a thick braid that almost always ended up in her mouth, and her eyes were like sandy blue tide pools, sometimes cloudy, sometimes clear. Harriet was the storyteller, the singer, and the second mother. Even though she was younger than Daniel, she had appointed herself Lord High Chaperone. When parents were absent, what Harriet said almost always stood.

Circe was asleep on Harriet's shoulder. Her eyes were

golden brown, her pearly blond hair was chopped in a sharp line above her jaw, her laugh was quick and never quiet, and she could only keep serious when she was sleeping.

Hyacinth may have only been a year and a half younger, but Circe's quick confidence made her feel incredibly small. Adults talked to Circe like an equal, and to Harriet like a superior. Both of the older girls were tall, bright, and unafraid. Like Daniel. Even Lawrence. While in any group, small or large, Hyacinth slipped to the back. She, the smallest Smith sister, the girl with the midnight hair and cool eyes, watched. She studied. She felt. She wondered. She noticed. But she rarely said what she had noticed, because she quickly doubted her own perception and made herself less sure than she was. Unless her sunny sisters dragged it out of her . . . and agreed.

Lawrence, only eight, writhed and grunted, then sat up, blinking. "Hy?"

"You're okay," Hyacinth said. "Go back to sleep."

Lawrence crossed his arms over the loose playing cards on the table and flopped his head forward.

A single fat drop spattered against the window, and Hyacinth watched its ruins run in a web across the glass.

She didn't know that she was watching the storm's final drop.

She didn't know why her parents were keeping a big

man tied up under a tarp in the back of the truck. And she didn't know that he had just kicked, shuddered, and taken his final breath.

As he exhaled, the ground shook.

The trailer suddenly bounced and slid toward the cliff, and the truck veered and accelerated, throwing tails of gravel, jerking the trailer hard inland, and the trailer skittered and swung and she fell backward and Lawrence yelled and the playing cards flew and Daniel and his sleeping bag slid toward her and Harriet and Circe both screamed and fell off the sofa onto Daniel's head. Half a mile of cliff was falling into the sea behind them. The roar muted the engine and silenced the wind and shook the very world. The truck and trailer roller-coastered up through walls of brush and slid through mud and stopped in a bed of drowning ferns beneath a massive old ten-trunked cedar with gnarled roots that looked strong enough to hold the earth together. Breathing hard, with her heartbeat thundering in her eardrums, Hyacinth rose to her knees on her cushion and peered out the rear window and saw the ruin and the wreckage of the coast and muddy waves romping over fresh stone and a whole forest of heavy timber being dragged out to sea.

She knew she had been the road's final traveler. Death had come close, and it made her feel cold to her core.

Harriet and Circe stood behind her.

Daniel kicked his way out of his sleeping bag and

hopped up. Together the siblings watched the ocean jump the rubble and test the new cliff with shattered spray.

"Everyone alive?" Harriet asked.

"I am," Lawrence said. He was wide awake and bouncing. "I'm alive. Can we get out and look? I want to climb."

"No," Harriet said. "No way." She pushed her braid back and turned to the front of the trailer. "I hope we aren't stuck. I so wanted a real bed tonight."

"We almost died," Daniel said. "Be grateful for any bed that isn't at the bottom of that cliff."

"And a shower," Harriet added. "Badly need. At least if I'm going to feel human again."

The door to the trailer banged open and Trudie Smith leaned inside, quickly scanning all five of her children with worried eyes. She, like Hyacinth, had dark hair and eyes like the moon in winter. Her hair was in a tight ballerina bun, and her skin was creased from wind and sun and work and worry.

"All present and accounted for?" she asked. "Anyone bleeding?"

"Yes ma'am! No ma'am!" Lawrence bounced up and down on the seat next to Hyacinth.

"That was interesting," Circe said. She shook back her short hair, more excited than scared. "It came out of nowhere. Was it an earthquake?"

"No. Just a lot of rain," Trudie said. "And then a truck pulling a trailer."

"You really think we were heavy enough to do that?" Daniel asked, but his mother was already retreating through the door.

"Sit down and grab on to something," she said. "This will be a rodeo for a bit."

The door banged shut and Lawrence slammed into Hyacinth, laughing, grabbing on to her arm. Hyacinth winced but didn't push her brother away.

"I don't know how one truck and trailer could knock that much cliff into the ocean," Harriet said. "Did you see all those trees?"

"We almost died," Circe said. "So what if it was the rain or the truck or an earthquake? My heart is still jumping."

Hyacinth opened her mouth to speak and then shut it again quickly. A thought had darted through her mind. But it was childish. Not something she wanted to share.

Harriet and Circe both looked at her. Harriet brushed her braid against her lips. Circe leaned forward.

"What is it, Hy?" Circe asked.

The truck engine roared and mud and gravel rattled against the windows as the trailer lurched forward.

Hyacinth looked out her window, watching brush and leaves scrape across the glass.

"Hy!" Lawrence nudged her firmly with his elbow. "What is it?"

"I was just thinking," Hyacinth said quietly. This was how it always went. They made her talk in the end, so she may as well say it now. "I was just thinking about the man in the truck. He might be why the cliff fell. We all know he isn't normal. Not by a long shot. Not like anyone else Dad has ever tracked." She looked at her older siblings. "Maybe. That's what I was thinking, anyway. I'm sure it was just the rain."

But she wasn't sure. And neither was anyone else.

"It's not like Dad is always tracking people," Circe said. "That makes him sound strange."

"He is strange." Daniel's voice was low. "We all are. And he's tracked enough. Whenever the Order needs help."

"I remember a few," Harriet said. "And all of them were . . . *wild*."

"Powerful," said Hyacinth. "Not just wild."

The trailer squeaked and bounced. Heads swayed with the motion.

Lawrence brushed the last loose cards off the table onto the floor and then stared at them. "But how could that man knock the cliff down?" he asked. "Dad shot him. And he burned his belt and his hair and tied both of his mouths shut."

"Yeah," Hyacinth said. "I know he did. We were just talking."

Two months prior and hundreds of miles away, Hyacinth's father had made an announcement at the dinner table. It was the same announcement Albert Smith had made to his children many times before at many different dinner tables. The Smith family was moving. The people who actually owned the house where they had been living would be returning soon. Albert had received a call or a letter or a telegram and another house was waiting for them, or one would be soon. There would be more overgrown gardens for the children and their mother to attack. There would be more lonely animals desperate for attention and training. More horses for Hyacinth to groom. More dogs for Lawrence to play with and Hyacinth to train. More engines for Daniel and his father to repair—trucks, motorcycles, boats, airplanes, and even one strange little jungle train with tracks to clear and a bridge to replace.

Hyacinth Smith had lived in wide-open villas with fountains and pools lined with hand-painted tiles as bright as the parrots in the trees. She had lived on desert ranches with one thousand longhorns, and in mountain lodges where the snow piled up ten feet deep. She had lived on the sand beside the Atlantic and on an island in the Gulf of Mexico. The Smiths had cared for run-down camps beside glacier lakes, had tracked down and recovered missing swamp mansions, and had tended huge houses in cities where no one spoke English. Hyacinth had lived like a princess and like a pioneer. She had slept on silk sheets and on piles of straw and on bunk beds with shrieking springs. She had studied the dolls and decorations of dozens of different girls, the family photos, the books, and she had wondered what it would be like to have a place of her own. A place where some other girl could stay and never quite belong.

Hyacinth could be comfortable almost anywhere, but she felt like she belonged nowhere.

The last house had been in the New Mexico mountains with stables bigger than any she had ever seen and a river rock fireplace large enough to hold a pitched tent. The horses had been well cared for, the dogs well trained, the house well cleaned, the gardens sparse but healthy. The job had been all for her father—two airplane repairs and one rebuild. So Hyacinth and her sisters had been able to read and write and dream and talk and laugh as the sun set in the evenings, and catch up on some of the studies their mother had planned for them.

And then a letter for Albert Smith—the first Hyacinth had ever seen carried by a pigeon.

And then the dinner table announcement.

And then goodbye to the horses and the landscape and the house and the gardens, and hello to the cramped trailer and the slow wander to somewhere else.

But this time was different. This time Albert hadn't even finished his job first. Not even close. Lawrence had bounced around clamoring for information on where they would be living next, wondering if the owner had sons, and if so, what age, and oh, would there be dogs?

"Two sons," Albert had said. "Eight and sixteen. Three daughters." He had crossed his arms and looked at his wife. "Gertrude, you remember the girls' ages?"

"I do." Trudie had smiled. "I ought to. Those three made their birthdays easy to remember."

"Wait a minute . . ." Harriet scrunched her brows.

"You're talking about us?" Circe asked.

"That's right," their father said. "Our place. Our very own place in California. That's where we're living next."

The girls had squealed and laughed in shock, and Daniel had grinned and picked up his still-smiling mother, and Lawrence had danced and made up a song about having a home and about never leaving ever not even when he was dead, but Hyacinth had known that there was more, and that it wasn't all good. She had known from the set of her father's jaw and the tension in his thick oil-stained fingers and the ring of hardness in his eyes that surrounded the happiness at their centers. She had known, but she had not said.

Hyacinth had looked carefully at her father, and he had understood and grabbed her tight and pulled her in under his arm and kissed the top of her head.

"Just one job first," he had said. "Shouldn't take more than a week or two. And then you get your own plants and your own dirt and your own little room and a shelf for your own books. Smile, Hy. Smile."

And she had.

Until the wanderings in Mexico. And the ghost towns in the California mountains. And the bodies. And then one night, Albert and Trudie had left the kids alone with the camper beside an icy river. And in the morning, they had returned.

An unconscious man with two mouths was bound and gagged in the back of the truck. He had been shaved, and his hair burned, and his black fur belt had been burned too, in case it had been charmed. And the kids had watched from inside the camper and the flames had jumped high and white and thunder had shaken the windows.

Albert, smiling, almost limp with relief, had told his children that it was time. Time for a home. Time for a place that would be theirs forever.

Hyacinth hadn't believed him.

OIL-STAINED HANDS WITH STUBBED nails and cracked knuckles lifted Hyacinth easily up off the floor. Her head draped over a broad shoulder, her arms swung limply at her sides, and her dreaming mind began to return to reality.

Her father was carrying her. The trailer door was open and he ducked carefully out into cool night air.

The sky was clear and the moon was high. Hyacinth could hear the ocean.

Albert set her down on buzzing feet but kept a hand on her shoulder as she blinked and wobbled. They were standing in a gravel driveway outside a big white house with boards over the upstairs windows. One light was on downstairs. Not far away, a decrepit barn was leaning steeply inland, missing chunks of its roof. A dim yellow light flickered above its door.

Hyacinth's mother held Lawrence with his blond head draped over her shoulder as she approached wide porch steps up to the front door. Daniel hopped up the stairs in front of her, while Harriet and Circe hung back, shivering.

Before Daniel could knock, the front door swung inward, leaving a screen door still closed. A lean shadow stood still behind the screen, holding a gun.

"Don't you move an inch," the shadow snarled. The voice was a woman's. "Who are you, and how'd you find this place?"

Hyacinth could hear the low rumbling growl of angry dogs.

Albert ignored the woman's instructions, jumping quickly forward.

"Albert Smith, ma'am," he said, and then gestured around. "My wife, Trudie. Our five children. No ill will

12

or ill intentions. I'm hoping we're at the right place. Who might you be?"

"If you need to ask, you don't need to know," the woman said. "What do you want?"

"Your finest pancakes," Circe whispered to her sisters. "Immediately. And fresh squeezed orange juice."

Harriet smiled. "A flat place to sleep will do just fine."

The girls were tired, Hyacinth knew. And for her sisters, tired always meant silly.

Albert raised his voice and his hands to hold the woman's attention.

"I'm old Isaac's grandson," Albert said. "I'm afraid when he passed, well . . . I inherited the place." He lowered his hands. "So that's why we're here. For the house."

For a long moment the woman was silent. Hyacinth expected her to say her name or maybe even claim that the house was hers. The still darkness made Hyacinth feel like another storm was coming.

And then, slowly, the woman pushed open the screen door, revealing three snarling low-slung dogs, built like muscled barrels with teeth.

"My name is Granlea Quarles," she said. "You're confused. This is *my* place, and I intend to keep it. You and your wife and your five offspring need to get yourselves elsewhere. Quickly."

Albert shook his head. "Ma'am, I'm sorry. I understand

this is unpleasant, and if I'd known someone was living here I would have written first. But I have the lawyer's letter and a copy of the will in my truck. If I could show you—"

The woman whistled sharply through her teeth.

The three-dog pack leapt out onto the porch. Daniel slid protectively in front of his mother. Harriet and Circe grabbed each other. Albert froze in surprise.

"Kill," the woman said. And the dogs exploded forward.

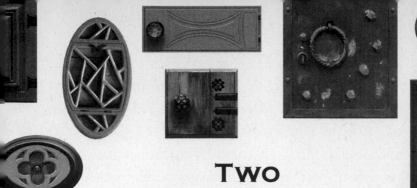

TWO

THE ATTACKING DOGS IGNORED Daniel. They parted around Trudie's legs, tumbled off the porch, slid on the damp, sandy path, ignored Circe and Harriet and Albert, and focused completely on Hyacinth.

Hyacinth bit her lip, but she didn't flinch or turn to run. Ignoring the adrenaline that pulsed through her, she didn't reach for her father, although he reached quickly for her. Hyacinth didn't let herself move at all. Not until the three dogs slid to a stop at her feet and sat their three rumps down in front of her with three tails thumping the ground and two tongues lolling.

Granlea Quarles stepped out onto the porch, staring at her dogs in surprise.

"Ray?" she asked. "Shark! Squid! Sick 'em!" But the dogs ignored the old woman, panting happily.

Relieved, Hyacinth dropped into a crouch, gently touching three cold noses, and then scratching ears. She shifted her weight on the uneven ground and focused on the biggest dog. In the dim light, he looked almost black, but she could tell that he was something closer to a stormy gray. And his belly was pure white. Old scars striped his muzzle.

"You must be Shark," Hyacinth said. She reached out for him, and the dog pawed at her arms with one rough foot. She scratched his gray shoulders, rubbed his white belly, and then moved on to the next dog. She knew that the old woman was unhappy. Hyacinth could hear sputtering, but she didn't care. She had a job to do, and her family was depending on her. If Lawrence had been awake and on his own two feet, then he would have helped. Animals deferred to him almost as much as they did to Hyacinth. But she had to handle this alone. The second dog was black with a wide skull and tightly cropped ears, but he had a white splotch on his forehead shaped like a stingray. And he held perfectly still. She leaned to kiss the splotch, and the dog smelled like hay and salt and long, dusty roads. She liked it.

"Hello, Ray. Lawrence will love chasing you," she said. "Yes he will. And now Squid . . ."

Squid was an old mottled brown dog with one brown eye and one that was such a pale blue it might have been blind. His fur was a little longer, and he was the only dog still keeping his tongue in his mouth. When Hyacinth reached for him, Squid inched away.

"Hey, now," Hyacinth said. She leaned forward, immediately sure that she was dealing with the smartest of the three dogs. "Eyes, Squid." The dog looked at her neck. And then at her hair. Squid was avoiding eye contact. Not an option, Hyacinth knew. The dog needed to belong to her pack, and he needed to know it.

"Squid, come!" the old woman hollered. "Come!"

"No," Hyacinth said quietly. "Stay."

Squid began to shake. He wasn't sitting anymore; he was forcing his rump down. And it took so much effort he looked like he might explode.

Hyacinth extended her hand, and Squid's eyes followed it. Then she moved her hand toward her face, and Squid's eyes slipped into contact with her own and then froze.

"Good boy," Hyacinth said. "Who's a good boy?" Instantly, the dog relaxed, and she grabbed his neck and scratched him under his collar until his leg thumped in happy reaction.

"Ma'am," Albert said loudly as Hyacinth stood back up. "Just because my girl has a touch doesn't mean I won't hold this little incident against you."

Granlea ignored Albert and studied Hyacinth. Hyacinth tried to smile, but her heart was thumping in her ears and the cold residue of fear was tingling all through her. Lawrence was fearless with any and all dogs. He didn't even have to try. Hyacinth had learned to bury her fear so deep that she forgot it until right after.

"How'd you do that?" the old woman asked. "What's the trick?"

Hyacinth looked at her father, and he nodded.

"Go ahead," Albert said. "You did good."

"No trick," Hyacinth said. "Just . . . a way to be. My grandfather taught me. I have scars from when it didn't work." She lifted her head and traced her fingernail in an arc beneath her chin.

After a long moment, Granlea nodded. "Well, I guess we can talk," she said to Albert. "And you can show me that will of yours. But I want my dogs back."

Hyacinth shrugged and looked down at Shark, Ray, and Squid, panting at her feet. She was pretty sure the dogs wouldn't chew on anyone, so they were free to do as they liked as far as she was concerned. All she really cared about was finding something to eat and someplace to sleep—as long as that place wasn't moving and it had enough room for her to straighten out her entire body. Even a concrete floor would be better than another tight night curled up in the trailer.

The inside of the house smelled like fish. And dog. But mostly fish. Fish with a serious smoking problem.

Hyacinth and her brothers and sisters followed their parents through a small entryway crowded with old rubber boots and hanging rubber slickers and heavy plaid wool coats. They shed their shoes and drifted into a living room unlike any they had ever seen—and the five of them had seen many. A single rocking chair faced a stone fireplace and chimney. An exhausted fire spilled black smoke out of the fireplace and up the face of the chimney, running along a dark stain stripe before pooling in blackness on the ceiling. It made Hyacinth think of waterfalls she had seen pouring down from rocky jungle mouths—but very, very opposite. Fire, not water. Upside down. Poisonous.

The rocking chair in front of the fireplace had been made from twisted and charred tree limbs. The seat and the arms were smooth and ruddy-gold with wear, but the rest of the chair looked like it could have been saved from a forest fire that morning.

Between the rocking chair and the fireplace, there was a solitary black-and-red Navajo rug on the floor, stained and torn. No couch. No coffee tables or lamps or shelves. But the room didn't feel empty. It felt . . . crowded.

Oddly sized door frames without doors lined the walls. Dozens of large picture frames—crudely planed, crooked, bent, burned in places—hung on wires across the empty door frames. Small frames were layered over everything— mounted with hooks, pegs, crooked nails, or tied in place with string and wire. Only the chimney and its smoky waterfall remained uncaged by empty frames.

Hyacinth turned in place. She felt surrounded by an army of emptiness. It was as if each frame opened on a tunnel to nowhere.

Circe gripped Hyacinth's arm. "New creepy room record?" she asked quietly.

"What?" Hyacinth blinked. For a moment she had forgotten that her siblings were right beside her.

"Oh, I think so," Harriet said.

"No way." Daniel crossed his arms, watching Granlea lead their parents off into the kitchen. "This isn't creepy at all. Weird, yes. But remember that ritual mask room in Panama? That was all nightmare."

Hyacinth looked at her brother, and then back at the walls. He wasn't wrong. She had seen creepier rooms, rooms dotted with ritual masks or voodoo dolls or ancient fertility symbols. But those had mostly told her something about the owners.

She walked behind the rocking chair, letting her hand graze its back. Rough. Dusty. Her fingertips tingled with the contact and she moved on to the closest wall, stopping in front of a wide rectangular frame that straddled two door frames and was in turn overlapped by three, four . . . six others, some of which overlapped each other as well. If she wanted to touch the wall, there were dozens of different paths for her hand to choose. She reached toward one and paused. Deadly cold trickled up her fingers as soon as her hand broke the plane of the first frame, and she flinched away. She shifted right and tested the next more cautiously. This time she didn't feel any shift in temperature. She felt . . . *pull*. Like her hand was steel and she was holding it over a hidden magnet.

"No touching!" Granlea yelled from the kitchen. "If

you touch, I won't be held responsible. And don't be sitting in my rocker!"

Hyacinth tugged her hand free, stepped back, and exhaled.

"Hy? What do you think?" Circe was right behind her. Harriet was farther back, pulling on her braid. Daniel still had his arms crossed. Lawrence wandered in from the kitchen rubbing his eyes.

"This is weird," Lawrence said, squinting at the empty frames. "Where are all the pictures?"

The grown-ups conducted their meeting at a small green linoleum-topped kitchen table. Granlea read over the will, then set it down and picked at her teeth before picking the will back up and reading it again. Albert and Gertrude Smith sat across from her, sipping at tap water in goblets of bronze glass. The kids claimed the floor. While the three dogs and Lawrence stretched out around and across legs, the elder four sat with their backs against kitchen cupboards and waited. With drooping eyelids and a warm swamp of dreams trying to pull her down into sleep, Hyacinth wondered how the evening would end. Would the old woman simply leave? Where would she go? Would she take the dogs?

What if she refused to go? She didn't think her parents would fight her for the house. Most likely they would end up back in the trailer, sleeping beside a highway, hoping for another wealthy family with another mostly unused house for them to tend. She was dreaming herself into that new house—made of stone and cedar beside a deep cool lake—when the old woman finally spoke.

"Isaac always was a fool," said Granlea Quarles. She slapped the will down, interlaced her fingers, and stared at Albert and Gertrude Smith. "Well, what do you intend to do with me? This was my brother's place, and our parents' before that, and now he's left it to you. I'd planned on dying here, but now I expect you'll want me to move along."

Hyacinth saw her mother grab her father's knee under the table.

"You were Isaac's sister?" Trudie asked.

"And I still am," Granlea answered. "Even though he's soil now. Buried him myself, one spot over from Stan, my husband. Always thought I'd end up between them." The old woman leaned back in her chair. Her white hair was still thick, and the light from the ceiling cast hard shadows across every crease on her face. The old woman's wrinkles looked like cuts that needed stitching.

"You can stay," Albert said. "For a while. How long do you need?"

"To die?" Granlea asked, twitching a smile. "Or to pack my things and move along?"

"Albert," Trudie said. She was wearing her sorry face. The one that she made for apologies and regrets. According to her sisters, Hyacinth made the same one whenever something bad happened, even if it wasn't her fault.

"She's family," Trudie said. "We can't throw her out. Did you even know you had a great-aunt?"

Albert nodded, looking Granlea square in the eye. "I knew. We met. And I heard stories."

"As did I," Granlea said. "And I remember young Albert here when he was just a fearless little lad who looked the spitting twin of that one sleeping on the floor with the hounds. He broke his wrist once, boulder hopping down the cliffs not far from here. Auntie Granlea was the one who set the bone. Brave boy didn't even faint. You remember that, Albert?"

Hyacinth saw memory heavy on her father's face. He rolled his right hand slowly.

"Albert," Trudie whispered, leaning toward her husband. "This is actually good. It could simplify things for us with the younger two. . . ."

And with that Trudie's eyes shifted to Lawrence, sleeping with the dogs, and then up to Hyacinth.

What? Hyacinth blinked, trying to question her mother with her eyes. What could Granlea Quarles, dangerous dog owner and gun wielder, possibly simplify for Hyacinth and Lawrence?

Trudie Smith didn't answer. But she made her sorry face.

"Upstairs was Isaac's," Granlea said. "Do as you will up there. But I'd appreciate it if you'd leave the front room and the barn to me. I sleep in that rocker, and I work in the barn. That's all I need."

"We'll need them both," Albert said.

"But not just yet," Trudie said, glancing at her husband. "Not immediately. Right? It will be a while."

Granlea smiled.

"Eventually, *Auntie*," Albert said, and his voice went so cold that Hyacinth wouldn't have recognized it if she hadn't been staring straight at him. "We'll be needing you to clear out of both. With no trouble and no complaint."

"But of course," Granlea said, her etched smile fading. "Whatever young Albert needs."

For a long moment the heavy breathing of three sleeping dogs ruled the room. Albert hadn't looked away from his great-aunt, and she remained motionless, returning his gaze with intense boredom. Trudie Smith finally cleared her throat and put her hand on Albert's shoulder.

"Do you think we could see the rooms?" she asked. "The children need to sleep."

Granlea Quarles didn't move.

"Auntie?" Albert asked.

The old woman slowly pushed back her chair and began to stand.

"We'll talk more," Albert said. "When the children are settled."

HYACINTH WAS STRETCHED OUT on an itchy orange plaid sofa positioned on the landing at the top of the stairs. It was an odd place for a sofa, but she preferred it to the cobwebby bedrooms cluttered with old dressers and pictures and mounds of dusty clothes spilling out of the closets. Of the four doors on the upstairs landing, Harriet and Circe were sharing a bed behind one, Daniel and Lawrence behind another. The third guarded the room reserved for the Smith parents, and the fourth stood open, revealing cold tile, a stained sink, an ancient toilet, and a tub and shower with no curtain.

Hyacinth twisted onto her other side, facing the stairs. The springs beneath her had sprung their last years ago, and the cushions exhaled mildew fluff with her movement, but with the pillow and blanket she had brought in from the trailer, the couch had still become her most comfortable nest in weeks.

Several miles beyond exhausted, Hyacinth should have been deeply lost in her normal dreams. But the strangeness of her surroundings had overwhelmed her weariness. Hyacinth couldn't sleep. She could hear Daniel snoring, and Harriet and Circe had stopped whispering an hour ago. She wriggled in place, sinking even deeper into the cushions. More fluff drifted and swirled across the landing, through the chipped white rail, and down the stairwell toward the only light that was still on in the house.

She heard the front door open and close, and footsteps moved beneath her toward the kitchen.

"I've never seen anything like him," Granlea said. "I swear it, Albert."

The old woman sounded afraid. Hyacinth held her breath and tried not to squeak a single couch spring. They were talking about the man her father had captured—the man with two mouths—and she had to hear everything.

"He came from somewhere near here and moved south," Albert said. "We were put onto his trail all the way down on the border." Her father paused. "How would something like that end up in California?"

Granlea's voice was low. "How do monsters end up anywhere?" She continued, but her voice drifted away. Hyacinth sat up quickly and leaned toward the stairs, peering through the light-striped rail.

"You have to know the stories I heard growing up," Albert said. "You and your brother were favorite villains around every campfire through every summer of my entire childhood."

"I was young," Granlea said. "And foolish. What are you suggesting? You think I created a monster? You think I summoned one? I haven't a spark of power in me, Albert. Not a spark. And if I did, I wouldn't be fool enough to use it. I wouldn't be fool enough to use it giving some blood-thirsty thug a second mouth or sending out invitations to nightmares. If I had the smallest kiss of magic, I'd register with the Order like a good girl and use it for hunting treasure or shaping a boat that would never sink."

"What are the frames for?" Trudie asked quietly. "The doorways?"

Granlea laughed. "Selling! An old woman's feeble craft, all made from lightning trees—novelty frames and doors and cupboards. You think I've been opening ways? Even my brother failed at that craft, and he nearly beat death itself. My husband died playing with Isaac's toys. Why would I try such a thing?"

"Boredom," Trudie said. "Loneliness."

"Insanity," Albert added.

Granlea sputtered loud frustration. "Why should I put up with this?"

"Because you have to. Where does an old woman find lightning trees?" Albert asked.

The old woman laughed.

"You haven't seen Mad Isaac's forest? Come with me."

Hyacinth heard footsteps moving toward the back of the house. She heard a screen door squeal and then thump shut against soft rotting wood. Throwing off her blanket, she jumped up and tiptoed quickly around the stairwell past the bedroom doors toward the bathroom—the only room upstairs without a board over its window.

Cold tile tightened the balls of Hyacinth's feet as she moved through the darkness to the glowing wisp of curtain that covered the high window. Standing tall and leaning forward, she moved the curtain just enough to make room for her eyes.

The glass pane was rippled and pearly white from years of blowing sand, allowing nothing but hazy moonlight through. No longer caring about stealth, Hyacinth pulled the curtain aside and felt for a latch. Her fingers found it, and the window slid up with a shove.

Cold sea air billowed into the bathroom around her, floating the curtain through her hair, sharpening her senses and sending a wave of goose bumps up her arms and down her back. Hyacinth leaned her head and shoulders out the window. An army of twisted and charred trees ran up the sloped valley behind the house. Vast trunks without canopies, candy striped with lightning scars and gouged by fire, lined with shattered limbs and crowned with dead splintered shards instead of towering life.

Even in the moonlight, Hyacinth recognized the silvery skin of eucalyptus, the sinews of cedar, and the bark and bulk of redwood. These had all been great trees once, she knew, kings and queens of their own groves. Now they slouched in aboveground graves, disfigured and dead— centuries wrapped up in each of them, centuries gathered into a rotting forest. Mad Isaac's forest.

Below her, Hyacinth heard voices. Human shadows moved among the monstrous shadows of trees, and she saw her father rest a hand on a cedar trunk while her mother hung back, turning slowly.

Behind them both, Granlea Quarles was ignoring the trees. Her face was turned back toward the house, and her white hair, fluttering in the breeze, was brighter even than the moon that lit it. She was looking up at the open bathroom window. She was staring at Hyacinth.

Hyacinth flinched when she found the old woman's eyes, ducking quickly back into the bathroom darkness. How long had the old woman been watching? How had she known?

Hyacinth leaned forward again, slowly. The old woman was waiting right where she had been, still watching. This time Hyacinth met her gaze and refused to look away. She was not going to let herself be afraid.

The old woman twitched a small smile.

Hyacinth didn't smile back. She raised her hands and slowly pulled the window down, leaving only a few inches open at the bottom. She wanted a sea breeze on the landing. Something to keep her thoughts calm while she waited for the sun.

The curtain drifted and danced as she backed away.

GRANLEA QUARLES WATCHED THE small opening in the upstairs window until she was sure the girl was gone. Then she shifted her attention up through the lightning grove to where the Smith parents were whispering to each other. She had known they were coming. She was even grateful—especially since they had managed to kill that double-mouthed nastiness when she had failed. She winced at the memory and rolled her shoulder. The deepest bites still hadn't healed.

Having Smiths around could be helpful if something went wrong like that again. But they weren't as simple as she had hoped they would be. Especially that girl. Any fool with half of one sense could tell that she was operating with something extra. She was a problem. Or maybe she was the best thing that had come Granlea's way in decades.

No reason to rush into action one way or the other. Not just yet. Things would become clear soon enough.

"Friend or foe?" Granlea asked. "What will it be, little Smith?"

Albert and Trudie Smith were walking back toward her between jagged trunks.

She flashed them a smile.

THREE

Hyacinth sneezed, sputtered, and sneezed again, kicking her only blanket off the orange couch and onto Lawrence's feet.

"Why are you sneezing?" Lawrence asked. "Are you allergic to here?"

Hyacinth sat up quickly. Sunlight was pouring onto the landing through the open bathroom door. Flocks of dust motes swirled around her brother's matted blond hair on invisible winds and weather systems.

"Dust," she said. "What are you—" She sneezed again. Violently. Lawrence laughed.

"Once," he said, "do you remember when I sneezed ice cream?"

Hyacinth shut her eyes for a moment and fought the tickle in her nose with the back of her hand. Finally, the feeling passed and she cautiously focused on her brother.

"Once," Lawrence said again, "do you remember when I sneezed ice cream?"

"I do," Hyacinth said, looking around. She swung her

bare feet onto the rough, dusty wood floor. Was anyone else in the house? She heard no footsteps. No voices. The bedroom doors were all open.

"It was in that ice cream parlor where Grandpa Jerry took us and I tried Pink Bubble Gum."

"I remember," Hyacinth said. "Served you right for ordering Bubble Gum." She could tell her brother wanted to relive the whole story, but she had no interest in reliving that or any other early childhood memories of bodily functions gone wrong. She stood up and felt her feet throb, once again adjusting to blood flow and body weight.

"I got pink all down my shirt and my chest was sticky and it sprayed out of my nose all over the glass case."

Hyacinth remembered it all vividly, and without any reminders needed. She grimaced and shook her head. The only thing she hated more than stories of bodily functions gone wrong were those moments when bodily functions actually went wrong.

"L, stop. Just don't," she said. "Please. Where is everybody?"

"I don't know. They got up, but I went back to bed. You were snoring out here and they decided not to wake you up." Lawrence shrugged. "Then you sneezed and woke me up."

Hyacinth groaned. "I hate sleeping. Hate, hate, hate."

"Why?" Lawrence asked. "I like sleeping."

"Drooling with people staring at you and you don't

even know," Hyacinth said. "Breathing weird and being all limp like an idiot." She was already moving toward the stairs. "Being asleep when other people are awake is the worst. Almost as bad as sneezing ice cream."

"I don't care about drooling," Lawrence said. "Or sneezing ice cream. But being awake is good too." He grew serious. "Awake, you can eat. And climb trees. And play with dogs and swim. And smell things."

Hyacinth paused on the stairs, looking through the landing rail at her sunlit brother. He continued. "But I dream about flying. So maybe sleeping wins."

"Come on, L," Hyacinth said. "Let's go."

She moved quickly through the bare living room lined with all the empty frames and headed straight for the kitchen.

"Mom?" The ancient green and mustard linoleum was sticky beneath her feet, and she peeled up quick steps toward the back door. Lawrence was still talking about sleep behind her as she pushed out onto a pair of rough-edged brick steps with decaying mortar. The sun was just high enough above the hills to have reached its full brightness, and low enough to be glaring directly at her above the groves of dead lightning trees.

Hyacinth squinted and shielded her instantly watering eyes. Light, like most things, affected her more intensely than her siblings. But she could already hear them.

"Why would anyone do this?" Daniel's voice asked

from somewhere in the middle distance. "So much work . . ."

"So much crazy," Circe said. "Totally bonkers. A forest of dead trees? It scares me that she's even family."

"Barely. But she's not the one who did all this," Harriet said.

"Yeah," Circe said. "Sure. Grandpa Isaac did it all by himself. Some of these look pretty new."

"Who cares about the trees?" Harriet said. "I can't believe Hy and L have to stay here with her."

"Maybe Mom and Dad are going crazy too," Circe said. "It makes me feel sick."

"Hey," Daniel said. "They wouldn't be doing it if there was a better option."

Lawrence nudged Hyacinth, and she jerked in surprise, opening her eyes. She had shut them without noticing, focusing on the awful conversation she was hearing.

"You asleep again?" Lawrence asked.

Hyacinth shook her head. She could see now, but she couldn't see her siblings. The voices were still there, but far more faintly. The dead forest filled the little valley that rose up behind the house and lined the slopes on either side, planted in crudely dug holes in strangely uneven and swirling rows, each blackened and splintered trunk beside a loose pile of earth. Live trees occasionally stood among the dead, and full groves with slowly swaying green canopies surrounded the valley. Hyacinth wanted to touch each lightning tree; she wanted to know every story wrapped in every ring from every day of every year that the gathered trees had witnessed. She felt like she was looking at the richest, most exhaustive library she would ever see—with every towering volume in a language she would never be able to fully read. But she had more immediate things to sort out.

To her left, a dozen yards from one corner of the grove, stood the battered barn. All its doors were shut.

"Where are they?" she asked her brother. "Do you see them?"

Lawrence pointed up the hill. One hundred yards and the first twenty uneven rows of charred timber separated Hyacinth from the conversation she had been hearing. She blinked, focused, and blinked again. There was Daniel, slapping a trunk and then poking at a black spiraling lightning scar at least a foot wide. Circe tucked back her short hair, stuck one leg forward, and crossed her arms. It was her best angry stance. Harriet was nervous, pulling at her braid.

"Should we go out there?" Lawrence asked.

"Hush," Hyacinth said. "Just for a second." And then she shut her eyes again and focused.

"Lots of families send kids to camps that young," Circe said. Her voice sounded like it was fighting through a breeze to reach Hyacinth's ears. "I know they do."

"And lots of families have money," Daniel said. "I'm surprised Dad can afford to send the three of us."

"Why should we have to train at all? What is a training camp even for? I just don't think they should split us up," Harriet said. "*Ever*. We can't let them."

"Let *them*?" Daniel laughed, but not cheerfully. "Let Mom and Dad? They're Mom and Dad. Do you think they want us taking care of other people's houses when we're all grown?" He was frustrated, that much was obvious. But not just at his sisters. He was frustrated that he had to be frustrated at his sisters. Frustrated that he had to defend a decision that he hated.

Hyacinth opened her eyes again, and the voices dropped to normal levels. Whatever was happening, Daniel hated it too. He hated it more than any of them. He was angry and even scared. But he was trying not to show it.

"What's going on?" Lawrence asked.

"Nothing good," Hyacinth said, and she grabbed her little brother's hand and pulled him off the loose brick stairs onto the gravel path. Already she felt alone with him—two kids on one life raft, floating toward something she didn't understand.

Hyacinth didn't head out into the trees. Ignoring her older siblings but still gripping Lawrence by the hand, she headed down the path toward the barn as quickly as her callused feet could carry her.

"Hy," Lawrence said, scrambling beside and behind her. "Hy! I'm wearing socks."

Hyacinth glanced down at her brother's feet. Much too large gray-and-red woolly socks were flopping off of his toes. Red stripes that would have been loose around a man-size calf were sagging around Lawrence's ankles.

Hyacinth skidded to a stop.

"I found them in a dresser." Lawrence looked down at his toes. "I didn't mean to wear them outside. They aren't mine."

"Go get some shoes," Hyacinth said. "Or just kick them off. I don't know."

Lawrence shuffled. "They look like flat sheep." He stepped on one flapping toe and then the other, tugging his feet free. He was wearing another pair of socks underneath, and they still had baggy toes, but they were white and much smaller.

"Are those yours?" Hyacinth asked.

Lawrence nodded.

"Good. Ruin them all you like. Now keep up."

The big barn had lost most of its paint on the seaward side, and its vertical wood plank siding was gray and bowed and tiger-striped with cracks. The metal roofing was entirely rust, and an old tractor with spiked metal wheels was parked on the barn's inland side.

At first, Hyacinth was focused on the large central door hanging on a battered but greasy rail, but as she and Lawrence approached the barn, she shifted toward a small door, slightly ajar on the seaward side. One of its hinges had torn out of the wall, and the other was hanging on by a single screw.

Hyacinth dropped her brother's hand and leaned forward, peering into the darkness. She was looking at stairs. And she could hear voices.

Carefully holding the door's weight so the hinge wouldn't have to carry as much, she opened it just a foot and then let the bottom rest on the ground. The screw held. She put her finger to her lips, warning Lawrence, and then slipped inside.

The cool dust of decades cushioned her bare feet as she stepped up onto the thick plank stair. Above her, she heard wings flutter and pigeons coo as they discussed some hidden roost. She smelled aging wood and forgotten animals and a residue of oiled leather and fuel and a long history of birds. And something recent and nasty—sour. Old meat. Blood. Death.

Daylight striped through the cracked siding and across the leaning stairwell. When Lawrence stepped into the barn behind her, she began to climb.

The loft was vast, crowded around the edges with piles hidden by thick brown oilcloth tarps that were themselves coated with dust and painted with pigeon blight. The center of the floor was open and protected by teetering and broken rails. A voice Hyacinth didn't recognize rose up into the rafters.

Hyacinth crept across sagging boards toward the light. The soft dust beneath her feet was now punctuated by dry pigeon waste, too densely sprinkled to avoid. The guilty birds fluttered in the rafters above her. She stepped over one owl pellet, and then two.

"Hy," Lawrence whispered behind her.

She flashed him a warning look, but he ignored it and pointed at the proof that a much bigger owl had been using the barn as well—pigeon skeletons picked completely clean and left to dry, with only the feathered wings left undamaged and spread wide. Lawrence was nudging the nearest winged skeleton with an absolutely filthy socked toe. Hyacinth knew that Lawrence would make even more noise if she didn't acknowledge his find, so she widened her eyes in brief amazement and then raised a finger to her lips.

Lawrence put one hand over his mouth in apology. Hyacinth crouched down, placed her hands palm flat in the dust, and eased herself forward until she had her first view of the lit floor below.

There was sawdust everywhere and stacks of partially milled lightning timber, and dozens of incomplete or damaged frames leaning against walls and hanging from hooks on the ceiling.

In the center of it all, a big man built like a picture-book Viking, with thick blond hair and a blond beard both well on their way to white, was crouching beside a body on a tarp, taking measurements with gloved hands and a large pair of metal calipers that looked like a giant earwig's pincers. The skin on his long, thick arms was sun-dark and speckled, and he wore his pants tucked into high boots. Hyacinth had never seen him before, but she had seen his type. Whenever men like him had appeared at the Smiths' different temporary houses, her father had always treated them like his bosses while the kids had steered clear.

The body on the tarp looked mostly normal from Hyacinth's perch—long brown hair pooling around the head, eyes closed, normal mouth slightly open, skin perfectly smooth and undamaged, even though it had now turned gray and looked slick with moisture.

"The head, hands, and feet are all well above average," the man said. His English was polished and easy, but he had an accent Hyacinth couldn't place.

"I would think you'd be more interested in the second mouth," Albert said, stepping into view. Trudie Smith appeared next to her husband, tucking her hand nervously under his arm and leaning against him. It was not a pose Hyacinth saw often. Whatever was going on, her mother needed comforting.

Albert continued, "And of course there's the fact that nothing seemed to injure him."

"Until he died, that is," the big man said.

"Sure," said Albert. "But even then I think that was more by choice. He was just tied up in the truck. And there are no wounds on him, even though I shot him more times than I can count."

"Well, he's rotting quickly now," the man said, and he slid his right hand under the corpse's neck, lifting up so the head fell back with a sound like a sigh.

And there it was—the second mouth.

Hyacinth caught her breath. Her mother had told them about the two mouths, but she hadn't seen them for herself. Under the chin, where the jaw met the neck, there was a wide seam of thin lips. The lips parted as the head flopped back, revealing upper and lower rows of small translucent teeth—teeth guarding the dark gaping entrance to the throat.

The man with the beard began to measure and count teeth quietly. When he finished, he lowered the neck back down, hiding the mouth, and rose to his full height.

"Bag, please," he said, pulling off his gloves, and a lanky young boy with dark skin stepped into view, holding an open black leather bag. The boy couldn't have been older than Lawrence, but Hyacinth was surprised at how serious he was, at how confident he seemed standing beside something so dead and monstrous and rotting. Or maybe she was reading him wrong. Maybe he was terrified but masked it well. No. Her first reaction was usually the right one. Beneath the confidence she didn't see fear. She saw sadness, and anger, and something harder than hard at the core—a pressurized seed of strength that could grow him into an unbreakable man, or blow him apart before he managed to become a man. The boy almost frightened her more than the body.

Lawrence had quietly joined her at the edge of the loft. Now he nudged her, whispering, "He looks fun. I like him."

Hyacinth almost laughed out loud. Clearly, her brother could see things that she could not. The boy looked fun to him, and that was that.

The big bearded man dropped his gloves and calipers into the boy's bag, then took it out of his hands and stepped back, gesturing for the boy to take a look.

"Go ahead, Rupert. Tell us what you think."

The boy circled the body slowly.

"Now what's the point of this?" The voice belonged to Granlea Quarles. "I've seen enough." Footsteps echoed across the plank floor below.

"Ms. Quarles," the bearded man said, "you will kindly hold your tongue and stay where you are for the time being."

The footsteps stopped.

The boy named Rupert clenched his fists and scrunched his face in a final moment of thought, and then addressed the bearded man directly with a playground British accent.

"He's a big one, yeah? And he looks more human. But he's the same type as the other three."

"Three?" Albert blurted in surprise. "Where were the other three taken?"

"One north," the bearded man said. "One east and well inland, and one climbed aboard a freighter five miles west of here. Yes, five miles out at sea. You understand, Albert, why we needed your assistance in the south. Our hands were full." He focused on the boy. "What have we learned, Rupe?"

"Skulls minus brains—full of fluid and slime. Skin and muscles made of something like super-tough, fast-growing tree fungus. No nerve endings at all. Grown by someone, controlled by someone, and then abandoned to die and rot off to slime."

"Or controlled by some*thing*," the bearded man said grimly. "I don't know anyone capable of growing mind-less double-mouthed nearly indestructible hunters from fungus."

"Fungus!" Granlea strode into view and nudged the gray body with her foot. "Fungus? This thing is a mush-room? Well, that explains the dogs paying the body no mind."

"I don't understand," Trudie said.

"We rarely do." The bearded man stepped forward. "How could we?" Together, he and the boy flipped the tarp up around the body. "Don't bury him, just on the off chance that he could reanimate in soil. Fire will do the

43

trick if you steer clear of the smoke. Might be best to just heave him off the cliff and let the tide take him."

"But where did this thing come from?" Trudie asked. "Why was it here?"

The bearded man shook his head.

Trudie finally pulled away from her husband. "Do we at least know what it was hunting?" she asked.

"By the end," Albert said quietly, "anything that moved."

Hyacinth exhaled slowly. The monster under the tarp had erased her earlier fear and replaced it with another. She was no longer thinking about what her siblings had been talking about as she'd listened to them walking through the lightning trees. She wasn't thinking about being left with Lawrence, or about camps or training or money. She wasn't even thinking about the living room full of empty frames.

She was thinking about how much awful, twisted strength it must have taken to grow a living, man-shaped hunter like the one wrapped in the tarp below her. Hyacinth Smith—who by the age of ten could coax life back into a dried houseplant with just a few morning touches and whispers, who could, almost by her mere presence, turn a greenhouse crowded with decay into fruits and flowers in a single month—couldn't even comprehend how much raw and brutal force would be required to shape any fungus at all into any shape at all. She wouldn't even know how to try. Fungus was explosive, hidden in rot, a celebration in decay. Fungus was practically uncontrollable.

Well, she thought, *clearly not for someone.*

Someone very, very powerful.

Someone who needed or wanted brutal, mindless hunters.

Lawrence was still peering over the edge, but Hyacinth slid slowly back out of view, rose to her knees, and focused on breathing evenly. She needed to think.

Instead, through the light rising from the floor below, deep in the shadows where the barn roof met the far wall, she saw a boot. The boot rose to a knee, and a boy was leaning forward over that knee with the sloping barn roof just above his sloping back. A long knife hung loosely from his hand, and his filthy face was almost an exact match to the shadows around him. But his eyes had too much light for any shadows, and as Hyacinth looked directly into them, she saw the boy flinch in surprise at having been seen.

Hyacinth could have yelled in surprise or fear. She could have jumped to her feet and run in panic. Most people wouldn't have blamed her. But she would have blamed herself. She swallowed and focused on another shape in the shadows, stretched out on an old horse blanket—the dark profile of another boy lying motionless on his back. He was sleeping deeply, or he was dead.

"Lawrence Smith!" Trudie Smith's voice rattled in the rafters. "What do you think you're doing?"

Lawrence jerked back much too late. Bashful, he looked up at his sister.

"Sorry, Hy," he whispered.

"Go," she said, but she wasn't looking at him. "I'll follow you."

As Lawrence hopped away toward the stairs, kicking pigeon skeletons as he went, the boy in the shadows raised a finger to his lips. Hyacinth watched raw intensity in his eyes. She saw desperation. He wasn't threatening her, but his look was clearly a command, not a request.

Hyacinth wasn't sure what she should do. So she did nothing. She didn't nod. She didn't acknowledge. She made no promises of any kind. Whoever the boy and the body were, they had no authority over her.

Turning away, she followed her brother to the stairs.

She didn't look back.

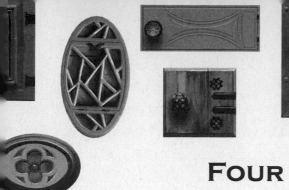

FOUR

THAT NIGHT, THE SMITH family sat down for a meal of chicken, potatoes, and tension.

Albert and Daniel had knocked a dozen wasp nests off two ancient plank picnic tables and dragged them out in front of the house so they could watch the sun set into the Pacific over supper. No one liked the idea of staring at the dead lightning forest while they ate. For tablecloths, Trudie had used old bedsheets, and camp plates and cups had been brought out of the trailer to make enough place settings. Chickens had been discovered by Harriet and Circe out among the charred trees, and a bag of dubious potatoes had been pulled out of a cupboard. Hyacinth and Lawrence had scrubbed every single one of them in the old porcelain sink while Lawrence talked happily of monsters and Hyacinth's mind wandered in urgent circles with no clear destination.

She thought about her father's strange jobs for strange men, the long hunt for the fungus man, and the cliff collapsing just behind them as the storm was ending. She thought about Granlea and the lightning trees and her siblings talking about leaving her behind and the barn and the boys hiding in the loft and the dead body and the two guests who had come to examine it. Which made her think about her father's jobs and the constant strangeness of the men and the Order he worked for, which took her back on the hunt for the fungus man, which placed her back in the trailer, which carried her back up the coast in a dying storm as the ground began to shake and the cliff began to fall.

So she turned, and so she never seemed to arrive. Who were the Smiths, really? Who was she? What was she for?

When the potatoes had finally been peeled, her knuckles were bleeding in four different places, and she didn't even notice.

The meal was the sort that Hyacinth would have normally savored—not for the food, but for the moment, for the scene, for the history of the occasion.

Yes, her mother's chicken was nearly perfect and the gravy was plentiful and solemn and the potatoes were creamier and more poetic than any spuds Hyacinth had ever met. Butter laughed beneath sea salt, and gravy anointed them both.

They were seated around two picnic tables that stood end to end in front of a sunset on the sea.

But only hours before, Hyacinth had watched her

father and a big bearded man poking and prodding a dead monster.

Yes, Albert Smith opened a bottle of wine he had been saving for eight years.

But there were two boys hiding in the barn, and one of them was hurt. Or dead.

Yes, the Smith family was sitting down for their first meal together at a home that was theirs.

But also for the first time, the Smiths would be separated. Harriet and Circe both had red eyes—Circe was angry, and Harriet was sad. Trudie looked exhausted and stunned, with hands scalded from cooking. Daniel had his head down and was barely eating.

And they were eating with two strangers who had come to see the monster, and a crazy old lady who clearly knew something about it but was refusing to talk.

In a family spun from laughter, only Lawrence was happy, and he was secretly feeding three dogs chicken under the table while making faces at the serious boy with the British voice.

Albert Smith raised a glass of wine. The wind rustled his hair as he rose to his feet, looking down the length of the tables at his wife. Hyacinth watched her mother sigh, tuck back her hair, and cross her arms.

The big bearded Viking was the only person at the table who immediately raised his own glass.

"A toast," Albert said. "On this momentous occasion."

Hyacinth picked up the yellow glass of ice water in front of her, its surface slick with condensation. Her siblings, even Lawrence, did the same.

"Bad luck!" the Viking said, and he set his glass down and clambered free of the table, grabbing the wine bottle as he did. Without asking permission, he grabbed Hyacinth's water glass, chucked its contents, and poured her a swallow of wine before doing the same for her siblings.

His name was Thor, and Hyacinth couldn't even pronounce his Norwegian surname. She supposed people named Thor who were as large as he was became accustomed to doing as they liked without asking.

"All right, then," Thor said when he had finished, and he tugged his beard and bowed.

"Albert . . . ," Trudie said, eyeing her children's glasses.

"It's fine, Tru," said Albert. "It's good." He looked around the table at his children, and Hyacinth saw more uncertainty in him than she had seen in a long time. As hard as his surface was, she could see intense emotion just beneath it. She could see it in the twitch in the creases at the corners of his eyes, in the tightness of his hard unshaven jaw, in the quick bounce of his Adam's apple, and in the way he looked at each of them, settling on her the longest, before refocusing on her mother.

"Smiths," Albert finally said. "We raise our glasses to your mother. She gave me the five of you. She gave me a life. In all of my drifting, she has bound us together, kept us sane, and kept us close—to her, and to each other." He paused, and all the children looked at their mother. Trudie wiped her eyes quickly and forced a tight-lipped smile. "God knows," Albert continued, "I haven't given her much in return."

Trudie shook her head. "Don't talk like that. That isn't true."

"Oh, yes, it is," Albert said, and he paused, collecting himself. Hyacinth had never seen him like this, and she knew her siblings hadn't either. Daniel and Lawrence had turned to stone. Harriet and Circe were both wiping their own eyes.

Thor the Viking seemed uneasy. He was now staring down at his plate. Rupert did the same.

As for Granlea, chewing loudly, she helped herself to another serving of chicken and stretched across the table to snatch the gravy.

"For years," Albert continued, "while I took us from house to house and place to place, your mother held us together. Now that she finally has a home of her own, we will be scattering. But I know, even scattered, she will keep us all close."

The wind surged, lashing the tablecloths like flags.

"To Tru!" Albert said, and he drained his glass. Thor and Granlea drank with him. But none of the children touched their glasses.

"But why?" Circe asked. "Why scatter at all?"

"It's only two weeks," Albert said. "For now."

"Your father and I are citizens of a unique society," Trudie said. "There are opportunities and benefits that exist nowhere else. And rules. Expectations. Duties. If our children make no effort at all to participate in our society, then we will be cut off, and all of those things vanish. Your father's jobs. The inheritance of this house."

"Children need to leave their parents," Albert said. "And you are talented children. You will accomplish great things and then come back to us, and we will sit here by the sea and listen to your stories. You will all surpass me. In everything. That is my prayer."

"But who is leaving?" Lawrence asked suddenly. He climbed off the bench and walked to his mother. "Where am I going?"

"Mr. Thor will be taking Daniel, Circe, and Harriet to a camp for a couple weeks," Trudie said. "Then they'll come back here for a bit, and then we'll take them to a huge estate on Lake Michigan for their real training. It's where our Order is headquartered. And it's where your father and I will be going for a couple of days, to explain about that mouthy monster and to finalize our ownership of this house. Mr. Thor will be kindly flying us in his airplane."

"So I'm staying here?" Lawrence asked. "Alone?"

Trudie put an arm around her son.

"No," she said. "You and Hyacinth will be here. Together. With the dogs. And Ms. Granlea."

Lawrence looked at Hyacinth with wide eyes, his dirty freckled face full of worry. She tried to give him a smile, but she couldn't. A smile would have been a lie.

"But I want to see the headquarters," Lawrence said, his voice rising. "And I don't want Daniel to go to camp. Can I go with him? Can I go to camp?"

"I'm going," Rupert said, and Lawrence stared at him, shocked by the injustice. "But my parents are dead."

Lawrence began sputtering and Circe launched into an interrogation of her father and Harriet pressed her braid against her lips and Daniel slowly stirred his potatoes and Hyacinth downed her wine with one gulp, blinked at the warm bitterness that flooded her mouth, and then stood up, taking her mostly full plate with her.

"May I be excused?" she asked her mother. "Please?"

Hyacinth felt her mother studying her face, looking for anger or sadness or disrespect. But Hyacinth knew that none of those things were there. There would be confusion, and there would be impatience to be somewhere else. She hated conflict. And she had more than enough things to process on her own. Trudie nodded and then hugged Lawrence, telling him that he was not allowed to cry.

Hyacinth turned her back on the sea and the sunset and climbed the stairs onto the porch, entering the house quickly, ignoring the empty frames and hurrying into the kitchen. In the kitchen, she scraped the dregs of the potatoes directly out of the pot onto her plate, and then she grabbed a mostly carved chicken carcass out of the roasting pan and set the whole greasy thing on top of the potatoes.

Then she slipped out the kitchen door, not letting it bang behind her, and hurried down the path toward the barn. She was wearing shoes this time, and she moved as quickly as she could without dumping any of the food off the plate.

As she reached the barn door, the three dogs swooped down the path behind her, slobbering and panting. While Shark and Ray let their tongues loll happily, Squid put his ragged ears back and growled at the barn.

"Hush," Hyacinth said, and she squeezed into the darkness and began to climb the stairs with the three dogs behind her.

At the top, she paused, waiting for her eyes to adjust. Light was no longer coming up from the floor below, but red stripes of sunset filtered through the cracks in the walls.

Shark and Ray snorted around the dusty floor until they were both sneezing on pigeon bones. Squid sat beside Hyacinth, with his ears up and his nose high.

"Hello?" Hyacinth moved across the loft, giving the hole in the center a wide and cautious berth. "I brought food. You must be hungry. I can look for medicine."

She stopped, staring into the shadows where she had first seen the boy.

Nothing.

Careful not to dump the food, Hyacinth crouched and moved all the way back to where the roof met the low wall. Squid put his nose down and snorted past her. An old horse blanket was rumpled on the plank floor, and Hyacinth could see that it was blackened with blood, some of it still slick.

Squid lifted one paw and pointed at it cautiously.

"Where did they go, Squid?" Hyacinth backed away until she could stand upright. The barn loft was completely empty, and the disappointment she felt surprised her. Her life had enough strangeness to it already—no doubt Circe and Harriet were both being emotional at her parents right now, and Granlea was obsessing over lightning trees and planning to make more empty frames, and the Viking man named Thor was insisting that Albert and Trudie get on a plane as soon as the dishes were done. Or maybe before.

She wasn't wrong. She knew she wasn't. So why had she wanted the two boys to stick around so much? With everything else that was going on in her life, why did meeting them and asking for their story matter so much?

Hyacinth didn't know. It was easier for her to understand what other people felt and why, easier to be outside looking in, not inside looking out.

Squid had already descended the stairs and vanished by the time Hyacinth slipped back outside. The sun was all the way down now, but the sky and the sea were still glowing. Up the path behind the house, Thor and Hyacinth's father were attempting to have a private word.

Hyacinth shut her eyes and leaned back against the barn, holding as still as she could, listening through the breeze.

"Of course she's more than old enough. Even the youngest is old enough. Rupe will be at the camp and he's just as young. Make me understand, Albert. What will I say to the Order? What will you say?"

"She can't," Albert said. "Lawrence would be fine, but not Hyacinth. She would hate it, and it would hate her. I won't do it. She's . . . sensitive."

"You'll have to someday," Thor said. "If she's so weak, she'll wash out quick and that will be that, no harm done."

Albert groaned in frustration. Hyacinth knew the sound well, and she knew what it meant. Her father didn't want to say something. And he was about to say it anyway.

"Not weak, man," her father said. "Not at all. She might be the strongest of us. Sensitive, as in, *sensitive.* Let me put it this way . . . when Hy was six, we had been reviving a ruined estate in Virginia, a place she especially loved because of an ancient oak alley planted by John Smith himself."

Memory flooded through Hyacinth as she listened. She was with her sisters, running down a grass track beneath the grandest, greatest canopy of limbs she had ever seen. The light through the leaves dappled the ground like a green and gold pony, and the wind above and around her sounded like the ocean. So many games happened beneath those trees, so many dreams. . . .

But her father was still talking, still explaining *her* to a stranger. She pushed the memory away and listened.

"Nine months later," her father was saying, "we were in a place she didn't enjoy nearly as much—a dry prairie ranch without trees. At the dinner table, Hyacinth announced to the family that it was time for her to use her stick to improve the place, and she pulled a dry oak twig from her pocket that she had been saving to make another oak alley. We all laughed and explained about acorns, and she just looked at us, confused. That night, she went out, and while we watched, she snapped that twig into the tiniest bits she could manage, and she tucked each bit into a little finger-deep hole, humming and chatting to herself all the while, lining the dusty drive on both sides."

Hyacinth opened her eyes and focused on her father. He was shaking his head in disbelief. The Viking was slowly pulling at his beard while he listened. Albert's voice was fainter, but she could still make out his every word.

"One week later, that drive was lined with saplings, and

my little Hy visited each of them every day. Each week, they laid on growth that would normally take an oak a full year, and each week that drive became more beautiful. Six months later, we left behind oak trees that looked at least thirty years old for some thrilled owners, and I had to lie like a villain to protect my daughter, taking credit for every bit of it, spinning tall tales of impossible transplanting. I've been in high demand ever since, and every place we've gone she's worked her magic, even when she doesn't know it. And every place we've gone, I've been terrified that someone in the Order will find out and take her from me."

Albert sagged and ran both hands through his hair.

Hyacinth bit her lip. Hearing the story like that was terrifying. She remembered it so naturally. She could make green things grow and change . . . *quickly*. But the way her father had just described her, she sounded—

"Magic," Thor said simply.

"No," Albert said. "I mean, in one sense, yes."

"You, Albert Smith, are telling me that your daughter is a witch."

Albert snarled so hard that Hyacinth flinched against the barn.

"No. Absolutely not. And if you ever use that word about her again, I will strangle you myself, do you understand me? Witchcraft is charms and spells and manipulations. My daughter has a gift, an ability given to her by the one who knit her together in her mother's womb."

"If it is a gift," Thor said, "then why do you fear the Order? Why must she be hidden?"

Albert laughed. "Because we both know their Burials are full of men and women with *gifts*. Because people like you will use the word *magic*. Because she will end up condemned because she is a bird with wings that enable her to soar, and the flightless will put her on trial and call her unnatural. She's the reason I've always remained distant from the Order. And I have worked for years to keep her off all membership rolls. She isn't completely erased from the records, but most of the official documents list only four Smith children."

"I noticed," Thor said. "I would have corrected the oversight on my return."

"Don't," said Albert. "The Order isn't for her. That's why she will not be attending any camps. That's why she will not be going to Ashtown with her sisters in the fall. I would appreciate it if you would remember this conversation, and I would appreciate it even more if you would immediately forget."

"Albert?" The voice was Trudie's. She was leaning out the kitchen door. "If we're leaving tonight, there's much to be done. Most important, find your daughter. Talk to her. Take her for a walk."

The kitchen door banged shut, and Albert refocused on the big man pulling his beard.

"I will remember," Thor said. "And I will try to forget."

"Thank you," said Albert. "And I hope you know that I can't be in Ashtown long. Gifted or not, my daughter can't stay with this woman indefinitely. Give me your word, that after forty-eight hours, you will fly me home no matter what the concerned committee might want."

"She will have her brother," the big man said. "I can make no promises."

For a few minutes after the two men left, Hyacinth stayed exactly where she was, with a cold plate of chicken and potatoes in her hand. The picnic tables were carried back around the house. She heard the clinking of dishes, and her mother singing a song as she washed them, the song that she had always sung to calm her children when she was actually the one in need of calming.

And then, while the darkness deepened, Hyacinth saw something moving out in the lightning trees. Squid appeared from behind a tree, looked her way, and then disappeared again. He reappeared, looked her way, and then redisappeared.

Hyacinth took a long breath and finally stepped away from the barn, but not toward the house. She was walking out into the lightning trees.

She didn't feel gifted. She just . . . noticed things other people missed. So she had noticed life in an oak twig when everyone else had missed it. So what? She hadn't put that life in there. She could never do a thing like that. No one could. She had just . . . invited it out.

Like right now, as she moved between the lightning-scorch-carved trunks, she wasn't putting all the roaring power inside them. She wasn't binding the rootless trees all up with storm rage until they were ready to explode.

Someone else had done that.

Hyacinth only noticed.

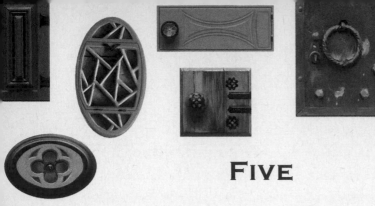

FIVE

SQUID WAS HOPPING AROUND a pile of sandy dirt beside a massive sinewy cedar. He wasn't barking, but his tail wasn't wagging either. As Hyacinth wove her way toward him, she could see that the tree had been struck with rot long before it had been struck by lightning. Deep inside the coiled lightning scar that striped the trunk, the wood was dark and as soft as soil.

A stick spun through the air over Squid's head and tumbled to a stop a dozen yards away. Squid dashed after it, scooped it up in his teeth, and returned with his head high and rear end wagging.

Hyacinth froze in place, watching. The dog dropped the stick and a hand stretched out of the shadows and picked it up. Squid bounced eagerly and turned in a quick circle. Once again, the stick flew.

"Good dog." The voice was young—a boy's—but already it was low and somehow, to Hyacinth, it sounded serious enough to belong to someone very old.

After a moment, she moved forward, and slowly the

boy came into view. His hair was black, unwashed, and matted. His jaw was hard, his brow and nose were sharp, and his skin was pale where it wasn't coated with dirt. He was shirtless, seated with his back against the cedar trunk beside a huge hollow in the wood the size of a small cave. With one hand, he was pressing an orange dishrag from Granlea's kitchen against a mess of blood and dirt high up on his shoulder, and with the other, he was playing fetch with Squid.

"You were in the barn," the boy said, and Hyacinth flinched. She had made no noise. She was downwind. She was out of his peripheral vision. Squid hadn't even acknowledged her approach.

The boy turned his head and looked straight at her. In the day's last light, the sharpness in his eyes tore right through her. He might have been younger than she was, but that didn't matter. She knew, in the first instant of that single look, that this boy saw even more than she did. Always. In everything. Everywhere.

Hyacinth swallowed, holding the plate in front of her with two hands, like a useless bumper that would never keep her safe in a collision. She shouldn't be here. She should run, find her father immediately.

But she didn't want to. Not until she learned more.

"These trees," she said. "They're strange." It's all she could manage.

The boy stared at her. After a moment, he nodded.

Hyacinth moved forward while he watched her. "I brought some food, but you weren't in the barn. Where's the other one?"

"The other one?" the boy asked. "You mean my brother?" He looked at the plate in Hyacinth's hands. "He will return."

Squid settled down in the dirt beside the boy, staring hopefully at the stick.

Hyacinth chewed on her lip and then quickly made herself stop. "My name is Hyacinth, by the way. Hyacinth Smith."

"I am called Westmore," the boy said. "Mordecai Westmore."

"I've never met a Mordecai," Hyacinth said. "Or a Westmore." She smiled and then immediately regretted it. It was the kind of thing Circe would have done.

"And I've never met a Hyacinth."

Hyacinth considered different possible responses to this. But none of them seemed intelligent. She almost described the flower she was named after, but decided against it. That's what Harriet would have done.

"Are you hungry?" she finally asked.

"My brother will be," said Mordecai. "He gave me everything he stole."

Hyacinth set the plate down beside him, and as she did, she couldn't help but smell the burned sourness of his wound—even beneath the rag—mixing with the rot that rose up out of the hollow in the tree. She wondered how Squid could stand it.

"What happened to you?" Hyacinth asked. "And how did you get here? There's only one road, and apparently at least one meadow flat enough for an airstrip not far from here. That's how Thor arrived, but you don't look like you have your own plane. A boat? Were you shipwrecked in the storm?"

For a moment the boy simply looked confused. Then he shook his head. "That is not your worry."

Hyacinth felt her confidence growing. The strange boy was making no effort to satisfy her curiosity.

"Well, you're on my family's land, and you obviously don't talk like you're from here, and you look like you're dying in our weird lightning tree forest, so yeah, it is my worry. What happened?"

Mordecai Westmore shut his eyes.

"We were hunted," he said. "We fled. I was wounded. And we lost ourselves here." He opened his eyes, looking up into Hyacinth's. "We are still hunted. My brother is lying in watch and wait. When more hunters arrive, he is hoping their path will show us how to return."

"That sounds complicated. And dangerous," Hyacinth said. "Where are you from? We have maps. My dad practically knows the entire globe. He could get you home."

Mordecai shut his eyes again and leaned his head back against the cedar trunk. He said nothing.

"At least show me your shoulder," Hyacinth said. "I can help. My mother could help."

"Tell no one of us," Mordecai said, his eyes still shut. "No one. Not your mother and not your father. Please."

Hyacinth didn't answer. Maybe she would keep a secret for this boy and maybe she wouldn't. It all depended on what else she might learn about who he was and what he was doing.

Slowly, wincing in pain, Mordecai peeled the rag up off his shoulder.

The boy had been bitten. Badly. The upper and lower jaw marks were obvious, even as they were surrounded by blood and blisters and oozing burns. But instead of punctures where the teeth had torn into him, large new teeth were protruding out of him.

Hyacinth knelt beside him and leaned forward. Not teeth. The protrusions rising up from the bite were something completely different. Two curved rows of hard fungus were growing out of the boy's shoulder, the kind that Hyacinth had only ever seen clinging to tree trunks. She let her fingertips touch them ever so slightly, and she immediately knew their urgent strength. They would not be easily removed.

Fungus. Growing out of a bite. In a boy. Her mind turned slowly as she tried to believe what she was seeing and incorporate it into the other strange things she had seen.

"You were in the barn," Mordecai said. "Did you see the hunter and his mouths?"

Hyacinth swallowed hard. She nodded. Now she was learning what those mouths could do.

"My brother tried cutting these out of my skin, but they grew back even larger. He cut them out and then burned the wounds with a hot knife. But they grew back again and now I am branded and blistered as well." The boy smiled slightly. "See? There is nothing you can do. There is nothing we can do but hope for another hunter to come for us, revealing another way home. If I can get home, my mother will be able to help me."

"Why another way?" Hyacinth asked. "Why can't you go back the same way? You haven't even told me how you got here in the first place."

The boy studied her face, hesitant. "Do you really not know?" he asked.

"How would I know something like that?" Hyacinth asked. "It has to be a boat, if I'm guessing. And the storm must have been awful. Was it smashed on the cliffs?"

Mordecai scraped his heel through gravel and looked at the looming grove around him. Even in the dusky light, Hyacinth saw the pain on his face, but there was so much more than that. She saw sight. And grief. The wounded, filthy, shirtless boy with the black hair and the sharp brows had lost more than she could measure—in addition to being lost himself. But on top of everything and below everything and all around everything else, Mordecai Westmore was frustrated. He was angry. Because he was not just lost; he was still losing. He was losing something more important to him than his own life. He was losing a fight, a fight he would die to win.

"You can see more than I can," Hyacinth said. "I can tell." She wanted to speak boldly like her sisters, but the words came too slowly for her to feel bold. She pressed on. "But I can see more than most people too. Should I tell you what I see when I look at you?"

The boy grimaced, adjusting the rag on his shoulder.

"Go back to your house." He grunted in pain. "If hunters come, it will be in darkness. And I don't want my brother to shoot you."

Hyacinth didn't move. She was seeing, letting herself focus completely on the boy in front of her. And what she saw was . . . extreme, yes, but so surprisingly normal it annoyed her.

Mordecai saw her annoyance and flinched in surprise.

"All right," he said. "What do you think you see?"

Hyacinth cleared her throat. "I see a boy who thinks it's time to die. A boy who would rather die than live and lose any more than he already has. You are confused. You are stupid—all boys are—but you think you're being so brave when you only want to quit. I have a brother who makes that same face whenever I'm finally beating him at Monopoly, and he suddenly decides he'd rather play something else so that he won't have to finish losing. You're hurt and you're lost and a girl wants to know where you're from and it's all so hard. You don't want my help. You don't want my mom's help or my dad's help. You say you want more of those monsters to come so that you can find your way home? I think you want them to come so that you can quit this game. After all, when you're dead, you won't know you lost."

Hyacinth was breathing hard when she stopped. She should feel sorry for the boy, but he made her angry, sitting there with his awful shoulder, acting too important to answer her questions.

The boy looked away. For a moment his jaw throbbed, clenching. "I don't know what Monopoly is, but something tells me that it's not like the game I'm playing." Anger burned on every word. "I would carry my fight into the grave and beyond if I could. I will not quit. I will not surrender. Ever. Not unless God Himself makes me." Scooping up a handful of dirt, the boy spat into it and then dragged the mud across his forehead. "I am Mordecai Westmore, seventh son of Amram Iothric, in the line long faithful to the Old King, and I swear it is true."

Hyacinth was silent, stunned. The way he spoke, and what he had just done ... it was all so old-fashioned. Otherworldly, even. Her eyes focused on the mud on the boy's forehead, and for a moment it seemed to flicker with purple and green fire, dancing with life. And then the fire was gone and all that was left was the mess on his head and the rot on his shoulder and the anger in his eyes.

Hyacinth shook her head. "You are very lost. And you need help. I should call my dad and bring him down here. He would know what to do."

"You're right, you know." Another boy stepped out from behind the wide cedar trunk. He looked identical to Mordecai in almost every way, but he was wearing a shirt and carried a bow over his shoulder and a quiver full of arrows on his hip. And where Mordecai's eyes were hard and his face serious, this boy's eyes spilled laughter, and his mouth seemed like it was barely containing a smile. "My brother is a quitter," he said. "It's because of his terrible burden."

"Be silent, Caleb," said Mordecai. "We don't know her."

"We know that she didn't tell anyone after she found us in the barn. We know that she brought us chicken." Caleb scooped up the plate and swabbed a finger loaded with mashed potatoes into his mouth. "And I know that she was right about you and losing. You're a quitter, Mordecai. This girl just called you a quitter."

Mordecai let his chin fall to his chest. "Stop," he said. "Please."

Caleb's face grew serious, but his eyes still laughed as they searched Hyacinth's.

"He's not really a quitter," Caleb said. "But he's very serious all the time, and now he finally has good reason to be. He's badly hurt, and I think being angry will help him fight harder."

"It will not," Mordecai growled.

"I disagree," Caleb said, and he crossed his legs, dropping onto the ground with the plate in his hands.

Hyacinth lowered herself down onto the ground facing the boys. As she crossed her legs, Squid snorted over to her and flopped his head onto her lap.

"Girl," Caleb said, chewing, "does your family have any enemies?"

"Her name is Hyacinth," Mordecai said, but he didn't look up.

"The Smiths?" Hyacinth almost laughed. "How would we have any enemies? We hardly know anybody. We've never lived in one place long enough."

Caleb stopped chewing and stared at her. "After watching your father, I knew your family had old wars. They weigh on him. And what you just said proves it. No matter," he added quickly before Hyacinth could object. "Our family has enemies."

"Enemy," Mordecai said. He finally looked back up at Hyacinth. "One enemy."

"And she," Caleb said, glancing at his brother, "has thousands who serve her. Whole nations. So we have enemies."

"She murdered our father," Mordecai said, and his words were like cold stones. They pressed against

Hyacinth's heart. "Brutally. She made a spectacle of him in her city square. Our cowardly allies knelt on his body, swearing their loyalty to her."

Hyacinth was barely breathing. She looked from one brother to the other. What they were saying didn't fit in the world she knew. But they were telling the truth. She knew they were. And she felt like a fool. The wounded boy was justified in his seriousness, in his sadness. And she had taunted him. He was hurt, and she had taunted him.

His father had been murdered? She couldn't even imagine that kind of pain. The story was like something from the Russian court. Or the mafia. She'd read about the first New York mobsters and the things they would do, and she knew people like that still existed.

But there had been a monster with two mouths.

And fungus was growing from the boy's wound.

Those were not things she understood. They belonged in the bedtime stories her mother would never let her father tell.

"Our older brothers are all gone too," Caleb said. "Killed or lost. We are the last two."

"We didn't think we could win," Mordecai said. "But . . ."

"But we had to fight," said Caleb.

"All we did was annoy the witch-queen," said Mordecai.

"And run," said Caleb. "It was madness. There were wolves and witch-dogs and wizards and dark faeren and hunters—so much barking and screaming and magic flying that it's amazing we didn't lose each other. Mordecai was tearing down walls and I was shooting at everything behind us when we crashed through into a garden full of twisted trees."

"It was a labyrinth," Mordecai said quietly. "A maze of arches and tunnels woven from living branches."

"And people," Caleb said. "People with their arms and legs grown into the trees, but we didn't have time to stop and wonder. The garden had guards. Hunters with toadstool flesh who were fully possessed by their mother, the witch-queen, the one who had grown them in some dark place."

Hyacinth's mind was swimming between horror and disbelief. These boys were not Russian. They were from somewhere well beyond her imagination.

Caleb looked at his brother, giving the telling of the story over to Mordecai as he chewed another bite of chicken.

"In the maze, we found seven open doorways, sealed with darkness only. Nothing was visible through them. Desperate, I chose one. We plunged through, thinking that we were entering some mysterious and twisted corner of the witch-queen's creation—a dungeon, a trap, a death sentence." Mordecai stopped his story and looked up at the dusky sky.

"And?" Hyacinth asked. "What happened?"

Caleb laughed. "We fell through an empty door frame, hanging on a hook in your barn, and landed in old hay. We had no time to be confused. Four hunters fell through after us. We fought our way outside, and my brother was bitten. Your dogs came to our rescue. The hunters have no minds of their own, and they were disoriented by this place. Perhaps their witch-queen mother lost her possession of them for a time. They scattered, one racing away to each point of the compass."

"First, they attacked the old woman," Mordecai said. "The dogs defended her, but she was bitten. It was not until she burned three with loud fire from metal tubes that they scattered."

"We hid," Caleb said. "But Mordecai was unconscious. I couldn't carry him far. So I watched the old woman—still bleeding from her own neck and shoulder—drag the doorway we had entered out of the barn. She chopped it up with an ax and then lit the pieces on fire. And I was relieved."

"For a while," Mordecai said. "It may have been a door into nightmare and the witch-queen's garden maze, but it was also our only way home."

Both brothers looked at Hyacinth, waiting.

"So . . . ," Hyacinth said. "A witch? A real one?"

"*The* witch," Caleb said.

"Nimiane, witch-queen of Endor." Mordecai spoke the

name quietly, as if the woman he feared might appear at the sound of her syllables.

"With actual magic?" Hyacinth asked. "Is she human?"

"By birth," said Mordecai. "But she is undying, as are all of her family's blood—blood indwelt by dark incubi. That is the source of her magic."

"I don't know what that means," Hyacinth said.

"And I don't believe it," said Caleb. "Demon blood or no, she is killable. She was born mortal, and so she will end."

A spotlight swept across the tree trunk above Mordecai and moved on to another, splattering bright light across peeling bark before vanishing again.

"Hy!" Albert Smith's voice rolled through the dead forest. "Hyacinth!"

Hyacinth gently removed Squid's head from her lap and scrambled to her feet. Caleb handed her the chicken plate, now bare.

"Say nothing of us," Caleb said. "Please."

"Hyacinth?" Albert yelled. "Are you out there?"

"Coming!" Hyacinth yelled. "I'm coming!"

Mordecai and Caleb were both looking at her, waiting for a promise, for assurance that she would keep the twin brothers a secret.

"No promises," Hyacinth said, and she stepped around Caleb. "And I'd put slugs on that fungus, not a rag."

The spotlight found Hyacinth before either boy could answer, painting her a ghostly blue shade of white. Squinting, she raised a hand to shield her eyes and made her way into the brightness, between the trees and over piles of loose sandy soil.

Her father was waiting between the house and the barn. Behind him, a gentle slope rolled down and away toward the cliffs and the sea. As Hyacinth approached, he lowered his flashlight, letting the brightness pool around his feet.

"How about those trees?" Albert asked. To his daughter's eyes, he looked nervous. Uneasy. And his smile was unconvincing. "There are easier things to collect."

"They make me sad," Hyacinth said. "The trees." The admission surprised her. As true as it was, she hadn't even noticed her sadness until the words came out.

Albert scratched at his unshaven jaw and studied his daughter as she stopped in front of him.

"Are you sure it's the trees?" he asked. "There's been a lot going on."

Hyacinth nodded. She didn't need to be more specific than that.

Albert sighed. If the trees made Hyacinth sad, she could see that she made her father sad. But which part? Leaving her? Hiding her from people like Thor?

"We need to talk," her father said. "But where? The

barn? You've always liked barns. Somewhere away from your sad trees."

"No," Hyacinth said. "Not the barn. The cliff. I want to watch the waves."

"It's getting dark."

"You have a light. And I have a lot of questions."

Albert nodded. Turning, he pointed his light toward the cliff and held out his other hand to his daughter.

Hyacinth set the plate on the ground and took her father's hand. Even though he wasn't a big man next to someone like Thor, his hand still swallowed hers up easily.

"There's a lot you need to know," her father said. "But only some I have time to say."

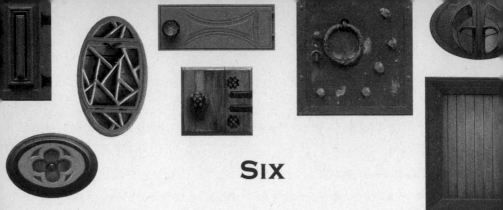

SIX

THAT NIGHT, MORE THAN an hour passed as Hyacinth and Albert sat and talked on a broken-down bench at the cliff's edge above a foaming high tide. It had been months since Hyacinth had spent a quiet hour alone with her father, and this one was peaceful—an hour in which every word mattered.

Which is why she couldn't stop reliving the scene . . . starting when Albert had flicked his light off, and together they sat in the cool darkness.

"Your mother and I will be back as soon as we can. Hopefully, this will be quick and easy. A day or two of explanations should make the Order happy. We'll be delivering the body, so that should help. It's not as if we'll have to describe it."

"And then the Viking will fly you back?" Hyacinth asked.

"The Viking?"

"Thor," Hyacinth said. "I don't know his last name."

Albert laughed. "Yes. The Viking has agreed to bring

us back. We'll drop Daniel and your sisters at a camp up north by sunrise tomorrow and then fly on to Lake Michigan. From there, we'll come straight back to you and Lawrence."

"And to Granlea," Hyacinth said. A large wave launched itself up the cliff and died, but cool mist found her face and she licked the salt off her lips.

"Yes," Albert said. "And Granlea. I'm sorry about her. And her forest of dead trees that makes you sad."

"They aren't dead," Hyacinth said. "That's what makes me sad. Most of the ones I touched still have so much life in them. More than normal trees, even. They survived lightning strikes and then she cut them down and they're just starving slowly in their holes."

"Starving?" Albert asked.

"No leaves to feed on the sunlight. No roots to drink or feed in the soil." Hyacinth looked up at her father's shadowy profile. "I might try to help them."

"It is our house now, Hy. And I would prefer a living wood to a dead one. Help them if you can."

A cold wind swirled up the cliff, and Hyacinth slid down the damp bench a little closer to her father.

He was wearing a rough canvas jacket that he had worn for as far back as Hyacinth had memories. It smelled of dirt and sun and motor oil, of fire and sweat and exhaustion. It held, for Hyacinth, the distilled aroma that was her father.

"You're gifted," Albert said. "And it's the kind of gift that would upset some powerful people."

"People in your Order," she said. "But what does the Order do? I know that lots of rich people with planes and houses are members, and they need people like us to tidy them up and fix things. But that's all I know."

"Do?" her father asked. "I'm not sure I understand you. What does a city do? A state?"

"You said the Order made you track down that monster, and now they're making you explain its rotten body to them. Dan and the girls have to go train for the Order, and I have to be kept secret from the Order."

Her father glanced at her in surprise.

"I heard you telling the Viking all about me," Hyacinth continued. "I know I'm not just staying behind to take care of Lawrence. He's actually staying behind for me."

"Hy . . . ," her father said.

"Just tell me what this Order is for," Hyacinth said. "Please. Especially since you're sure people in it won't like me."

Her father shrugged and sniffed at the wind.

"It was founded centuries ago to be a defense against monstrous evils that threatened or twisted the natural order. In the beginning it consisted of explorer monks who set themselves on a ceaseless quest to carry light into the darkness. They became collectors and caretakers, and when needed, conquerors and killers. Our family has been connected to the Order for centuries; your mother's too. I have never conquered, but I have killed. And when the evil is unkillable, it is collected and Buried, imprisoned and bound as permanently as possible. It isn't easy, but it can be done, even to history's biggest nasties." Albert Smith blinked against the wind and once again set to scratching his jaw. "If our double-mouthed monster had only died more quickly, your Viking might not have come to assess his carcass, and your mother and I wouldn't have been summoned to give a full report. But he survived so much, I thought he might be one in need of Burial. It doesn't happen often."

"So the Order is good," Hyacinth said.

"Well . . ." Albert scrunched his face. "Yes. But it is made up of people. And people can be the biggest monsters of all. Although they are more often just petty and selfish. Monstrous men do happen, but foolishness is more frequent. And it would be the fools who would misunderstand my daughter, the fools who would lump your gifts in with those who set out to destroy the world. I will keep you from those fools as long as I can."

"Do we have enemies?" Hyacinth asked.

"Enemies?" Albert said. "Us? Why would we have enemies?" He tucked his hands into his jacket pockets.

"The fools. Are they our enemies?" Hyacinth asked. "You know they would misunderstand me because they misunderstood you. Right? You're like me. You can tell."

With an explosion like muffled thunder, a wave shattered against the cliff, and spray rocketed straight up in front of Hyacinth and her father like a sheet.

They both ignored it.

"I am not like you," Albert said. "Not nearly. I have only a whisper of what you have."

The water kept rising. Mist swirled around them both on the bench.

"But you know what Granlea's doing with her wood," Hyacinth said. "You can sense that."

Albert rose to his feet. Seawater and foam began to rain down around him, but somehow it didn't touch Hyacinth.

"Obviously," Albert said. "Granlea is attempting to open doorways between worlds and times using the power contained in lightning trees. She has already let in two boys and four monsters, and if she is insane enough to keep trying, the Order will have her killed or imprisoned and all her wood will be burned."

"How do you know about the brothers? And what do I tell them?" Hyacinth asked. "Can they get back? How do I get fungus out of a person? I can help things grow, but I've never tried to make things die."

"I wish you'd asked me all of those things before I left," Albert said. "I wish you'd told me that you heard me talking about you and the Order. I wish you'd told me about the brothers and the door that they entered and the witch-queen who grew the monsters and the wounded boy's fungal bite, because I never would have left. I wouldn't be on the Viking's plane and Granlea wouldn't be attempting to open another doorway right now. I would be here to stop her." Albert backed toward the cliff. "But I am not."

Hyacinth jumped to her feet.

"Wait!" she said. "Don't go!"

"Too late," her father said. "I did. Make sure Lawrence changes his socks. Socks. Please. Fresh socks."

With that, Albert Smith stepped backward off the cliff, vanishing into an impossible torrent of water. The cliff shook and cracked. The bench and the ground began to slip into the sea.

And Hyacinth jerked awake.

Breathing hard, she sat up and scrambled backward on her itchy orange sofa, kicking her blankets onto the floor. They landed on Lawrence, who was snoring peacefully on the landing with one hand dangling through the stair rail.

Honest memory crept slowly back into Hyacinth's world. She had talked with her father on the cliff. He had told her about the Order and how long their family had belonged and how he was sorry to leave her with Granlea even for a couple days, and she had listened, but her thoughts had been on the brothers. On their story of stepping through an otherworldly doorway into the barn. On lightning wood and the strength she had felt in it.

She hadn't said anything to her father about the brothers or the fungus bite or their strange story of the witch-queen who had killed their father. And now she wished she had.

Hyacinth looked down at her brother, sleeping in a stripe of moonlight that spilled in from the open bathroom window. After the family's midnight farewell and departure with the Viking, Lawrence hadn't wanted to be alone. So he had dragged a pillow and blanket onto the landing to camp out on the floor beside the couch. Now Lawrence seemed to have flopped almost completely free of his bedding. His face was pressed directly against the old wood planks, and his arm was dangling down the stairs. Given the moist sputtering in his breathing, Hyacinth was sure that her brother was drooling.

As the dream adrenaline faded and reality settled in around her, Hyacinth lowered her feet to the floor beside her brother. She should wake him up and drag him to a real bed. Or at least get his pillow back under his head. She slid off the couch and knelt on a pile of blanket beside Lawrence. Peeling his sticky face up off the floor, she quickly tucked the edge of his pillow back under his cheek. And as she did, a hot wind rose up the stairs and inflated around her, filling the space.

The wind smelled of tar. Of smoke. And its heat quickly became more than an enveloping warmth. It had edges like blades, frying every invisible drop of moisture out of the air. It pressed in against her, digging, testing every nerve on her skin.

Lawrence writhed, kicking the blanket tangle completely clear of his legs.

Downstairs, Granlea began coughing. And just as quickly as the heat had risen up the stairs, it was gone, replaced with slow, crawling coolness and the sound of rain.

Hyacinth left her brother sleeping where he was, and she tiptoed carefully to the top of the stairs and listened.

Rain. Rain spattering on stone. Rain spitting on leaves. Rain splashing in puddles, and finally, rain drumming on a metal roof. Hyacinth heard it all, but the sounds were coming from downstairs, not from outside.

The floor beneath Hyacinth's bare feet shivered with the sound of distant thunder. Behind the house, barely audible to Hyacinth's heightened senses, the dogs had begun to whine.

Carefully, Hyacinth descended the dark stairs, stepping around the worn middles of the treads, trying to avoid squeaks and creaks. But the house was old and new to her and she couldn't avoid them completely. Every sigh and groan in the wood beneath her stopped her heart and briefly froze her progress as she waited to see if she had been detected.

Two-thirds of the way down, a hidden nail shifted in its hole. The stair tread popped like a knuckle. She paused in the darkness, holding her breath.

All around Hyacinth, the air changed again. Dank

heat crawled across her skin, like the air in a hot flooded basement. And then she heard the fluttering of wings. And cursing.

"No!" Granlea bellowed. "Wrong!"

Hyacinth heard the rocking chair bang in the living room, followed by quick footsteps. An uneven light flickered to life, and then there was a whoosh of something being swung through the air and a crash of something wooden falling.

A furry flying animal the size of a dog careened into the stairwell and slammed into Hyacinth, battering her face and hair with sticky leather wings as wide as an eagle's. Hyacinth threw her arms up and fell backward onto the stairs, too surprised to scream. The frantic animal clambered over her and flew over the landing, clearing the rail and then crashing loudly into the upstairs bathroom.

Hyacinth heard the shower curtain fall, rings and rod clattering into the old cast-iron tub.

And then silence. Lawrence was still breathing steadily. Hyacinth's heart was trying to break free of her ribs, and she'd bitten her tongue hard enough that her lower jaw was pooling with blood.

"Idiot bat," Granlea muttered. "I'll feed you to the dogs."

Hyacinth rose to her feet and descended the last few steps quickly. Upstairs, she heard the giant bat scuffling in the shower curtain. The noise made it easy for her to slip down the short hall and lean into the living room.

Granlea Quarles was on her hands and knees picking up pieces of a broken picture frame. Her rocking chair was tipped onto its side, and a kerosene camp lantern was on the floor beside it, along with an old broom with a dinged and bent yellow handle.

While Hyacinth watched, Granlea rose to her feet and threw the broken frame pieces at her fireplace, not appearing to care at all how accurate her throw might be. The broken pieces tumbled and hopped loudly, and Granlea stepped back into the center of the room, putting her hands on her hips and puffing loudly in the heat.

The old woman was wearing a black tank top, and her bare skin was spotted and loose and a shade of tan that made Hyacinth think of decay and age. Her white hair was in a bun, and at least four nasty rows of tree fungus teeth had erupted from the skin on the back of her neck and down both shoulders. It made her look like she was part dinosaur.

"All right, then," Granlea muttered. "No more playing around. Time's up, Granlea Agrippina Quarles. Time is more than up."

Hyacinth inched forward, gaining a wider view of the living room and the walls layered with empty frames.

Granlea moved to the wall beside the fireplace and

lifted a frame down. She grabbed another smaller one and carried them both across the room and stood in front of an empty doorjamb. Her hair twisted and fluttered, brushed by invisible movements in the air. Granlea hesitated, shivering slightly. Then she lifted the larger of her two frames and held it carefully centered in the empty doorway. After a moment Granlea let go and stepped back.

The frame floated in the air where she had left it. Hyacinth blinked, focusing every one of her senses on what she was seeing, trying to understand. The frame wasn't floating gently. It was trapped, being pulled in every direction with equal force. The wood strained. The seams in the corners stretched and expanded. And once again, the air completely changed in the room.

Hyacinth stepped closer, out into the open. But Granlea didn't turn.

Biting cold billowed out of the frame, breaking around the old woman in a swirl of frost, sparkling in the lamplight.

"Isaac!" Granlea yelled. "You daft old man, are you in there?"

Snow fluttered and spun across the plank floor.

"Well, if that's the world you chose, then you really are dead." Granlea snatched the frame back out of the doorway. For a moment the frame still blasted cold, swinging the old woman's bare arm up and around while it spewed the last of its frost and snow. But only for a moment. Granlea dropped it at her feet and gripped the next frame with both hands, examining its joints closely.

"I've been avoiding you," she said to the frame. "You know I have, and you know why."

The frame had a small opening, but the wood was wide and black on all four sides. At first, Hyacinth thought that it had been especially charred by lightning, but as the light flickered, she saw that only some of it was burned, but all of it was dark. The heartwood of a tree she did not know. A tree she did not trust.

Whoever made the frame clearly didn't trust the wood either. As Granlea turned it over in her hands, Hyacinth could see that it had been backed with golden plates, strapped and riveted at each corner.

And then, as if in a rush so she wouldn't change her mind, the old woman stepped forward, tossed the frame into the doorway, and jumped back.

The black frame snapped into the center, shivering with intense force, and the air around Hyacinth began to move again. But this time it wasn't moving toward her out of the frame. It was moving from behind her, flowing down the stairs and down the hall and breaking around her, rolling dust and frost across the floor, sucking it up into the air around Granlea's legs and swirling the collected mess into the dark frame and away out of sight.

The temperature dropped again, but not with blowing cold. It dropped because the heat was being stolen.

Hyacinth blinked, suddenly dizzy, queasy, cold at her very core.

"Name thyself."

The female voice curled and twisted around the room like a demented cat. Hyacinth wasn't even sure whether she had heard it outside her head or inside. She gagged and braced herself against the wall.

Granlea was turned a little sideways, like a boxer, with both hands raised in defense as her hair pulled itself loose, pointing at the empty doorway.

"Granlea Agrippina Quarles. I am mistress of this house, and I forbid your entry. I seek an old man named Isaac, lost between the worlds, I believe. Who are you? Do you have him?"

"There is only one world. And its many roads are mine." The voice sucked at the air, as if spoken by an inhaling storm. "And you, Granny, are no longer the mistress of this house. You cannot forbid me."

"I am, and I can," Granlea said, widening her stance. "Who are you? Do you have Isaac? If you do, I am willing to make you a trade."

Dappled light spilled out of the frame, and the sucking wind stopped. Pale gold and harsh quivering green spread across the floor, like sunlight on metal trees. The frame began to bend and twist slowly.

"No!" Granlea jumped forward, but a long-bodied white cat leapt up from beyond the frame and perched inside it, hissing. The animal's skin was wrinkled and nearly hairless, and its vertical pupils were glowing green. It looked from Granlea to Hyacinth.

"Your Isaac is dead," the voice said. "Killed by the bite that now kills you."

Granlea's head slumped, and she rolled her shoulder painfully under its mountain range of erupting fungus.

"I want his body," she said. "I want to see it."

"There is no longer a body," the voice said. "And you will suffer the same as your brother unless I heal you. What will you pay me?"

Granlea slumped to the floor and put her head in her hands. The cat leapt out of the frame, landing in the room, lashing its white tail and focusing its wide green eyes on Hyacinth.

Hyacinth slid back toward the stairs. She was about to vomit, and her skin had gone slimy and cold.

"The boys," Granlea muttered. "Those twins your hunters were after. They are still here."

Wood popped and the frame shivered.

"Yes," the voice said, and it sounded hungry. "I will take the boys. And the girl behind you as well."

"What?" Granlea looked up and around, seeing Hyacinth for the first time.

"The boys have angered me, and I will destroy them with agonies uncountable. But the girl." The voice practically purred. "She will be more useful."

Wood began to split. Metal groaned and stretched.

"No entry!" Granlea shouted. Jumping up, she kicked at the cat and then reached for the dark misshapen frame.

The wood exploded before she touched it.

The old woman tumbled. Splinters swarmed through the room like bees. Light haloed the tall shape of a woman standing inside the doorway. She might have been the most beautiful thing Hyacinth had ever seen. Her skin was both sun-kissed and silken. Her hair was black and weightless around her shoulders. Her eyes were emerald and pearl, but strangely unseeing, like the eyes of a perfect doll. The pale cat turned and leapt up into the woman's arms.

Hyacinth staggered backward, ignoring the tiny shards of wood that had pricked into her cheeks like quills. The woman was looking just over Hyacinth's head, but the cat in the woman's arms was looking straight into Hyacinth's eyes.

"I am Nimiane, heiress of Nimroth's undying blood, mother of incubi, goddess of worlds, witch-queen of Endor." She smiled at the hallway behind Hyacinth. The cat lashed its white tail across the woman's olive arm. "What is your name, girl? You are a grower and a healer, a waker of trees. Name your fathers to me."

Hyacinth swallowed. "I . . . ," she said. "My father is Albert Smith."

"A smith," the woman said. "Not a wizard? Is he not the one who bound the powers of lightning and crafted these doors? Is it not his blood in your veins that gifts your touch with growing things?"

"No entry," Granlea said from the corner. "You may not cross this threshold, witch." She managed to sit up. "Unless we agree to terms."

"Terms!" Hyacinth yelled. "No terms." She looked at the witch and then at the witch's cat. "This is my family's house, not hers. I'm the oldest one here, and I say you can't come in."

The witch began to laugh, and as she did, the purring in her voice vanished, replaced with something more like shards of glass rattling in phlegmy lungs. She stroked her cat and looked up at the ceiling, smiling. But the cat stared right at the old woman in the corner.

"What foolishness have you taught this girl, Granlea Agrippina Quarles? I am no faerie and no lesser imp, to be bound by threshold laws and charms."

With that, Nimiane, witch-queen of Endor, stepped through the doorway, passing from another world into the living room of an old house on the cliffs of the California coast. Every board in the house shook and popped. Dust rained down from the ceiling, and frames fell from the walls, clattering to the floor.

Hyacinth felt the earth shiver beneath the house, and she knew the lightning trees would be swaying and boulders would be slipping into the sea. The presence of the woman was like the presence of an entire city, like the movement and weight of a crowd all bound and contained in one shape. She was so overflowing with stolen life and power, Hyacinth felt as if she were standing beside a barely contained explosion.

"Hy?" Lawrence's voice echoed down the stairs and into the hall. Quick footsteps followed. "Hy!"

Before she could stop him, Lawrence tumbled into the hallway beside her and then stood, blinking, with mouth hanging open.

As the shaking of the house stopped, the cat purred.

Outside three dogs began to bark.

Behind the witch, a ring of seven barely animate mushroom men rolled and stumbled into the room, along with the intense aroma of rot and fungus. They were just as tall but far more slender than the monster Albert had killed, and they were grown together like one creature, each with what passed for its hands and wrists attached to the elbows of the one in front of it, with head bowed, eyes closed, and brow firmly grown into the skin between the next pair of shoulders.

Hyacinth grabbed Lawrence's hand and backed them both toward the stairs.

"Be still," the witch said. "Or your brother shall be devoured at my feet." She flared her nostrils wide and drew in a long breath. The light dimmed. Granlea cried out in pain and collapsed on the floor. Hyacinth gagged as she felt a ball of her own strength slip out from between her ribs.

The witch was collecting life from everything around her, but not for herself. With a light brush from her fingertips, the ring of mushroom men writhed and groaned. Backs arched, and foreheads and hands tore free of each other. Eyes opened wide, and mouths opened wider, yawning above and below pale jaws.

"Gather them all," the witch said. "And bind them in my garden."

Hyacinth didn't wait for the monsters to focus on her. Jerking her brother fully off his feet, she raced for the stairs, dragging him up behind her.

And the house was filled with snarling.

SEVEN

HYACINTH HAD NO PLAN. She had only instincts. Racing up the stairs, she managed to drag Lawrence beside her and then shove him ahead around the rail and past her couch.

Four mushroom men slammed into the stairwell, climbing quickly up and over and around each other like four parts of one creature.

Lawrence was yelling.

The fake men were snarling.

Hyacinth's adrenaline overflowed and her heart stopped in a chasm between beats. She froze.

The stair rail broke. Mushroom men careened over its ruin, slipping on Lawrence's bedding.

Lawrence shoved Hyacinth onto the cold tile of the bathroom floor, and as snarling gray men raced down the landing toward them, Lawrence slammed the bathroom door, turned the antique brass lock, and pressed his back against it.

Hyacinth blinked and gasped, pulling in a long, painful breath. Her heart was beating like a hummingbird's.

"What's going on?" Lawrence asked. "What do we do?"

Heavy bodies slammed into the bathroom door so hard that the panel bowed and paint cracked and flaked, raining down on Lawrence's shoulders.

"Out," Hyacinth said. "We have to get out."

Hyacinth looked out the window. She could see the barn with its dingy yellow light. She could see the dark army of lightning trees.

Behind her, the door began to crack. A fist exploded through the wood above Lawrence's head.

"Hy!" Lawrence yelled. "Help!"

Hyacinth threw the bathroom window open, grabbed her brother, and quickly boosted him headfirst onto the edge of the roof. She was a little wider, but there was no time for hesitation. Arms first and then head, she scraped her ribs on both sides as she wriggled out. Her hip bones banged and glass broke as she dove the rest of the way through, landing on the roof and practically sliding off the edge.

Lawrence grabbed her, and she pushed herself up onto her knees.

"Now what?" her brother asked, and he pointed past the gutter and over the edge of the roof. "That's rock down there."

They both heard the bathroom door crash off of its hinges.

As a gray fleshy head emerged from the window with nostrils flared, an arrow whispered past Hyacinth's ear and plunged in between the man's eyes, knocking him back inside.

"Move south!" Caleb yelled from the ground. He already had another arrow on the string and he drew its feathers back to his cheek. "It's lower there. Then dangle and drop!"

Caleb let his next arrow fly above her head, and glass broke behind her.

"C'mon!" Lawrence yelled, and he pulled his sister by the hand.

Doubled over and scrambling sideways, Lawrence and Hyacinth raced across the rough roofing with bare feet, making their way to the corner of the house lowest to the ground.

But it was still high.

"This is nuts," Lawrence said. "I wish Dad was here."

"No kidding," Hyacinth said. "Now how do we do this?"

"Hang on the gutter and then let go," Lawrence said. "And fall. And get hurt."

"Better than being eaten by mushrooms." Hyacinth rolled onto her stomach and slid her feet and legs back over the edge. All at once, her weight passed the point of no return and she felt herself teetering.

"I just . . . oh . . ." And she fell, just managing to hook her fingers in the gutter as she did.

Metal squealed and popped and tore away from the house, sagging two feet down before it stopped.

"Perfect." Lawrence was peering over the edge at her. "Let go, Hy!" And then his face went white. "No!"

Strong arms wrapped themselves around Hyacinth's legs and jerked her down. She screamed as the rusty gutter ripped free of her fingers and bounced up toward her brother.

The skin touching her was cold. And slick. And it smelled of fungus.

She kicked, but it was like kicking sandbags. She twisted and punched, and then long-fingered hands grabbed her wrists, pinning them to her sides.

Two mushroom men held her in the air between them. In unison, they rotated her slightly and she found herself eye to eye with one of the gray-skinned monsters.

His pupils flattened, wobbled, and then rose up into slits. Hyacinth knew that she was looking straight into the eyes of the witch even before the false man slowly opened his upper mouth and the witch's voice emerged. His jaw and lips were motionless, but the flesh in the back of his throat contorted and writhed with every puffing, trash-can-scented syllable.

"Grower girl, do not struggle. My sons will carry you to a garden where your gift will be honored among the gifts of my most favored slaves."

Hyacinth wriggled in the air, and the monstrous grips tightened on her legs and arms.

"Let her go!" Lawrence yelled from the roof above. "Put her down right now!"

The gray face looked up and then contorted into laughter so vile and rotting that Hyacinth's eyes burned and she went dizzy from the smell.

Her head lolled, and she threw up all down the monster's chest. Surprised, he refocused his attention on her.

She shut her eyes. The witch could look at her, but she didn't have to look back.

Green and purple light flashed through her eyelids, and a sound like a river chewing rocks surrounded her.

Hyacinth opened her eyes and saw the witch's shock in her slave's last look. But only briefly, because enormous grapevines, shimmering with light, lashed around the monster's head and shoulders and throat.

An army of living vines trailed behind the monster to where they all emerged in a storm of light from the palm of Mordecai's extended hand.

The wounded boy closed his fist, swung his arm around the light like he was gathering rope, and then jerked it all toward himself.

Arms were shucked from shoulders and fungal heads exploded. Hyacinth dropped to the ground in two huge piles of mushroom under a coiled and tangled canopy of ancient vines, all loaded with dark, heavy grapes.

Mordecai staggered forward, fell onto his wounded shoulder, and shut his eyes.

"Oh, my gosh," Lawrence said. He dropped off the roof, dangled on one of the thick remaining vines, and dropped to the ground beside his sister. "How did he do that? Who is he?"

"Mordecai!" Caleb fought through the vines and lifted his brother to his feet. "What were you thinking?" All three dogs trailed behind him, staying clear of the vines and every scattered piece of fungus flesh.

Hyacinth rose to her feet, blinking away her dizziness.

"Thank you," she said. "They had me, and then—"

"No time," Caleb said, turning away. "Come on. Quickly. Run."

Hyacinth tugged Lawrence along beside her, but not before he could grab a large cluster of grapes off the nearest vine.

Half carrying, half dragging his brother, Caleb raced straight into the lightning trees. As he passed beyond the first rows, Mordecai grew more stable on his feet, and Caleb shrugged him off.

"These trees," Mordecai said. "They give more strength even than the old faeren groves."

"Of course they do," Caleb said. "But that doesn't mean you can wield it. You could have used a tithe of that force to crush that pair, and then I wouldn't have needed to carry you out."

"I'm fine," Mordecai said, and rounding a gnarled old cypress tree trunk, he slowed to a stop and rested his palms and head against the scarred bark.

Hyacinth and Lawrence stopped beside Caleb. The three dogs lined up beside them with noses pointed back toward the house and ears and tails up.

"Who are you guys?" Lawrence asked Caleb. "And what is going on?"

Caleb looked at him and then at Hyacinth. He didn't answer. Instead, he pulled one of his final two arrows from his quiver and dropped to a knee beside the dogs, watching the house.

"She didn't lose her connection with her slaves this time," Caleb said quietly.

"I know," Mordecai answered, still leaning on the tree.

"She came herself," Caleb said. "She's here. She entered this world."

"Hy?" Lawrence asked. "Please tell me what's going on."

"Granlea's been using lightning wood to open doorways between worlds," Hyacinth said. "These brothers came through, chased by the first man with two mouths that Dad killed."

"Not a man," Caleb said. "And good for your father."

Hyacinth looked back at the house. They were only a couple hundred yards away, but they were shrouded in shadow.

"Not a man," Hyacinth repeated. "But he belonged to a witch who already killed their father, and she's been after them too."

"We're after her," Mordecai muttered.

"And now," Hyacinth continued, "she's come through Granlea's doors herself with seven more of her not-men."

"Seven?" Caleb sighed. "That's unfortunate. I hoped four was her favorite number."

Hyacinth looked at her brother. Lawrence was staring at her with his mouth open. Everything on his face told her that he was struggling to believe a word she had said, even though a real cluster of grapes was dangling from his hand.

"You saw what happened in the living room," Hyacinth whispered. "That was her." She nodded at Mordecai. "And you saw what he just did."

Lawrence looked at Mordecai and then at the grapes in his hand. "Are you a wizard?" he asked.

"Wizards are thieves," Mordecai said. "Like Nimiane, they steal power they were not born with."

"Our father hated them," Caleb said.

"Then what are you guys?" Lawrence asked. He held up the grapes. "Are these real? Can I eat them?"

Caleb smiled. "They are real. But they may be bitter. I am like you. But my brother is more. We were in the womb together, but I was the sixth born of her sons. He was the seventh. He is a pauper-son, a green man, born with the second sight—eyes that can see the living words of creation. In our mother's garden, beside a sea not unlike this one, an old vine was the first growing thing to reveal its burning word to him. I, a sixth, saw it too, but only faintly, like a ghost. But the vine fire blazed through my brother entirely, marking him from his palm to his soul and out again."

"Do not talk about it," Mordecai said, still not looking up.

"He was blind for a week," Caleb said. "But when the blindness passed, everything had changed for him."

Hyacinth moved to the tree, just beside Mordecai. She could feel the life somehow flowing between the wood and the boy like a draft in a room with no clear source. And then she placed her palm on the tree.

She felt the life inside it, woven into every ring; she felt it draining, drying. To her touch, the cypress felt like a house collapsing, like a barn crumpling beneath a century of winters that had all arrived in a single moment. It was like an insect being drained by a spider.

And the boy was the spider.

"Stop it!" Hyacinth said. "You have enough. You don't have to kill it."

Mordecai looked up, surprised.

"It's dead already."

"No," Hyacinth said. "It's dying, but it's still alive."

"It has no roots," Caleb said. "It's just wood in a hole

now. The witch would drain the life from a whole forest until it was just ash on the wind. My brother will only take what they don't need. This one doesn't need anything now."

"Yes, it does," Hyacinth said. "It needs as much as it can get." She focused on the trunk. There was still violence inside it from the lightning strike. A few branches were broken off above her head, but she knew that there were no roots below her. "C'mon then," she whispered. "Don't sleep so hard. There will be sun tomorrow. And then rain."

The tree couldn't hear her, because it had no ears. But it could feel her touch; she knew it could. She couldn't command it. She couldn't shape the life or the power she felt inside it, and she couldn't take it. But she could make suggestions. She could inspire. And she could wake.

There was more than enough energy in the tree to spread a canopy and shatter stone with new roots. It only needed urging.

The trunk groaned, and Mordecai stepped back.

"How did you do that?" he asked. Hyacinth retreated beside him. He was staring at her, studying her hands and her face. But she was watching the tree.

Ten feet above them, the broken branches twisted slowly, and then young shoots burst up from their bark, extending past the jagged crown at the top of the trunk.

The ground shivered beneath Hyacinth's bare feet. Mordecai looked down and then at her.

"Roots," she said. "Splitting stone."

"You're a witch," Mordecai sneered. "What spell was that? You have no faeren magic, or I would see it."

"Don't be stupid," Hyacinth said. "I'm not a witch, and I don't know any spells. I didn't do anything. The tree did. It used all the strength it has been collecting from our sun—our star—for centuries."

"That is not possible." The boy reached out and felt the trunk.

"It's a lot more possible than you throwing vines out of your hand."

"I don't throw them," Mordecai said. "I gather any strength I can. Because a vine was the first to touch me, the force emerges—"

"Guys," Lawrence said, pointing toward the house. "Look."

"Be silent," Caleb said. "Be still."

"I don't throw vines," Mordecai whispered.

"Stop," Caleb said. "We need a plan."

Hyacinth crouched behind the three dogs beside her brother. Shapes were moving out from the house in both directions. Many shapes. Dozens. All fanning out around the lightning trees.

"I guess only seven hunters was too good to be true," Caleb said.

Hyacinth recognized the glossy shapes of the mushroom men, but there were others too. Men in cloaks and high boots. Men with bows and men with swords and men with staves like scythes, crowned with long hooked blades.

"Those aren't just hunters," Mordecai said. "She's brought her witch-dogs."

"Witch-dogs?" Hyacinth asked.

"Wizard warriors," Caleb said. "Her thralls. She feeds them powers they are not strong enough to gather for themselves."

"We should hide," Lawrence said. "Where can we hide?"

All three dogs began to growl, and then Hyacinth saw the wolves. They had to be wolves. They were much too big to be anything else. There were three of them, and they were perfectly white, brighter than the moonlight. Each wolf was held back by chains, held by two men, one on each side.

"Whoa . . . ," Lawrence said. "Those are really big dogs."

"Wolves," Caleb said. "We can't hide from them. We'll have to fight through."

"Through to what?" Hyacinth asked.

"To the doorway they just entered inside the house," Mordecai said. "The doorway that will lead us back to our own world."

"You're nuts." Hyacinth shook her head. "We have to get out of here. Right now. We have to run." She grabbed Lawrence, pulling him to his feet and backing away.

Three stripes of pale orange fire surged up from the house and over the lightning trees, touching down on the other side.

Hyacinth blinked in the sudden light. The fiery rainbows hung in the air, shrinking the shadows between the trees to almost nothing.

"Where do we go?" Lawrence squeezed his sister's hand tight. "Hy. Where do we go?"

Hyacinth pulled him behind the cypress tree, leaning out just far enough to keep her eyes on the house.

Mordecai and Caleb slipped behind a tree across from them. The dogs held their positions, still growling, but quietly. They knew they were outmatched.

Beside the house, the witch-queen stood tall in the leafy tangle of Mordecai's vines. She extended both hands and the vines disintegrated, swirling in ash around her feet.

"There she is," Hyacinth whispered. "Shoot her, Caleb. Do something!"

Caleb didn't move. Mordecai was saying something in his ear.

NIMIANE, DAUGHTER OF NIMROTH, witch-queen of Endor, shut her eyes and sniffed at the salty air. She did not care for the sea. Almost as much as she did not care for the green men. The sea was unwieldy, even for her. But the green men were worse than unwieldy. They were self-confident savages best devoured young—younger even than the one she now hunted. In Endor and its many territories, seventh sons were enthralled or destroyed at birth. Even as thralls, the green ones often found their own minds and rebelled.

But when they developed a hunger and desire for the devouring power she could offer them, a green man could not be surpassed by any wizard. And all of hers had been killed by the vile Amram Iothric. The boy might be worth tempting, if only to further spite the memory of his dead father.

Her mushroom sons and slaves would be in position soon. And her wolves would hunt. But if she could shorten the fight, she would. She let her mind wander behind the eyes of her sons, moving her senses from one skull to the next, looking down at the firelit graveyard of trees. They were perched on rocks and in brush, waiting to attack, but they saw nothing.

She hadn't expected them to. With a slight shift, she felt for her cat.

"Bast." With her eyes still closed, she hissed the animal's name under her breath. When the cat was close, she didn't need to. But over distance . . .

Nimiane's mind was filled with orange light. She was crouched low, moving like liquid between thick tree trunks in holes and over mounds of loose earth between them. She smelled rodents. Rats had filled almost every crack with their scent. She wanted to pursue. To capture and torture, to pierce flesh and taste heartbeaten blood, but she could not. She was Bast, and she was hunting larger prey.

The cat slowed, lowering her belly almost to the ground. The breeze was coming to her, and it carried the smell prints of four hated people. Three hated dogs.

Fifty more strides and her eyes found them. She dropped all the way to her belly, moving nothing but her tail. With it, she lashed the wind.

A girl people and a smaller boy people of the same blood. Another boy people with weapons and a boy people wearing his soul on the outside—a soul of greens and purples that twisted and wound around him like dancing snakes.

Three dogs. Two were simple brutes. But the third dog, the ugliest, wore his soul on the outside, just like the boy people. The dog's soul looked like clear steely tongues wavering around it like bladed water.

His soul wouldn't matter. The wolves would eat him whole regardless.

"We stand ready, Queen." The words came through different ears in a different place, but the cat heard them clearly.

"Yes," Nimiane said. "We do. The children have not yet reached the center of the wood. Strike now, and gather me the green boy."

"Which is the green?"

The boy people wrapped in fire. The cat hissed. She wanted her queen to crush the fool and let Bast lick the hot blood.

Nimiane silenced the urges of the cat. Bast would stay and be her eyes.

"The one tearing your body apart with vines or shattering your bones with wind," the witch-queen said. "He will be the green. Bring him to me still drawing breath."

"Strike!" the man yelled, and chains rattled loose in front of the witch. Clawed feet tore at the earth as the wolves raced away. The shouts of men echoed between the hills, but Nimiane did not open her eyes. The excitement would happen elsewhere, where she was already watching. She felt fear and anticipation trickle up Bast's spine.

HYACINTH WAS TRYING TO think. Fighting was not an option. As amazing as Mordecai's vines had been, he had collapsed after destroying just two of the mushroom men. But running didn't seem like much of an option either. They needed to hide, and they needed to hide right now. From wolves and men and monsters and a witch-queen with her crazy cat.

She could hear voices. A man's. And then the witch's.

"Hy?" Lawrence was squeezing her arm. She tugged it loose and put her hands on her head.

"We have nothing," she said. "What do we have? Nothing. A couple boys and three dogs."

"Hy?" Lawrence grabbed her again. "Look."

"We have boys and dogs and . . . we can't just hide behind trees."

She looked at Mordecai and Caleb. Caleb had an arrow on the string, and Mordecai was breathing deeply, clearly preparing for his final fight.

"Death is a vanquished foe," Caleb said.

"Death cannot end me," Mordecai answered.

"Stop it!" Hyacinth hissed. "We are not dying right now! We are not!"

"Hy!" Lawrence pinched her arm tight. "Look!"

Finally, Hyacinth followed her brother's glance. Fifty yards away, at the base of a huge cedar with a gaping trunk, she saw the witch's white cat. Its belly was low, its eyes were glowing from the firelight hanging above them all, and its tail was lashing slowly.

"She's watching us," Hyacinth said. She turned back toward Caleb and Mordecai. "The witch knows where we are!"

Caleb shrugged. Mordecai's lips were moving. He was praying.

"Squid!" Hyacinth whispered. "Here!"

The mottled dog broke formation with the other two and trotted to Hyacinth. Dropping to her knees, she grabbed his head, pressing her own against his, pointing his snout at the cat and the gaping cedar tree.

"You see it?" she asked, and the dog tensed.

"Strike!" The witch-queen's command spread out over the trees. Hyacinth heard the chains rattle as the wolves were loosed. War cries and shouts washed around her from all sides. Shark and Ray were both whimpering, but Squid was undistracted.

"Kill," Hyacinth said, and the dog rocketed toward the cat.

"They're coming," Lawrence said, picking up two rocks. "Hy, they're coming."

Caleb stepped out from behind his tree, drawing his bow to his ear.

Hyacinth grabbed one of Lawrence's rocks and threw it hard. The stone hit Caleb in the ribs. Gasping, his arrow flew astray and he wheeled on her, furious.

Hyacinth jumped up to her feet.

"If you two don't come with me right now, I'll kill you myself."

Turning, pulling her brother beside her, Hyacinth raced after Squid.

The cat was gone. The dog was gone. But the cedar tree with the gaping trunk was right where it had been. She could wake that tree, just like she'd woken the other one. And that meant she knew where to hide.

Or where to die.

Maybe.

Hyacinth didn't know if the brothers were following, and she almost didn't care. She and Lawrence sprinted up and over a mound of loose earth and slammed against the big damaged trunk.

"Inside," Hyacinth said. "Quick." And before her brother could ask a question or complain, she shoved him into the dark hollow and heard him yelp as he dropped inside. "Coming!" she warned, and she hopped in after him, sliding down charred wood and rot and landing on earth at the bottom of the hole, more than four feet down.

Her head and shoulders were above ground level. Outside she could hear the cat yowling and Squid barking and wolves snarling and men yelling. But she couldn't watch. There wasn't time. She had to focus on one thing and one thing only. She closed her eyes and placed her forehead and palms against the damaged wood inside the tree.

"Please," she said aloud. "Please mend your skin. Live again, and hold us."

"Hyacinth!" Lawrence screamed.

But she couldn't look. She couldn't let herself feel anything but the life inside the tree.

The wood trembled against her palms. Rot rained down around her shoulders.

HYACINTH DIDN'T SEE CALEB kill the first wolf with his last arrow. She didn't see Mordecai throw the second wolf over the cypress tree. She didn't see Ray and Shark nipping at the third wolf's heels, distracting it from the two brothers as they ran.

She felt the tree waking and wood growing as centuries stirred beneath her touch.

And she felt Caleb's boots as they slammed into her shoulder and knocked her sideways.

She banged into Lawrence and opened her eyes as Caleb fell into the hole and pressed them both back as far as he could.

Mordecai stood outside, facing away from the tree, guarding the entrance, a long knife in one hand and his other blazing with vine fire.

The tree groaned like a ship at sea. The crack was closing.

Caleb tried to climb back out to join his brother, but Hyacinth grabbed his shoulders, pulling him down and slipping past him.

"Get in here!" she yelled, and then, from between his boots, she saw what Mordecai was facing.

The tree was surrounded. With a sweeping lash of light and vine-muscled wind, he sent six mushroom men tumbling, all twelve mouths raging. With a snap of his arm, crossbow bolts bent around him, and as the wolf and the men with scythes approached, he slammed his fire vines against the ground, roiling a wave of shattered rock toward them, pounding them against the trees.

And through all the noise, Hyacinth could hear him humming. And she could feel his exhaustion. His boots slipped. He slumped forward and caught himself on one knee, just in time to brush a flying scythe up into the trunk. The snarling wolf leapt forward, and he swept it back, but only barely.

The men saw his exhaustion, and for the first time, they began to smile.

Sweat was pouring off of Mordecai, and while the vine fire around his hand still burned bright, his skin had gone gray.

The crack was closing.

"Let me out!" Caleb jerked at Hyacinth's shoulder, but she kicked him back and lunged up and out of the hole, grabbing onto Mordecai's boots.

The tree trunk pressed against her ribs and spine.

Caleb didn't need to be told to pull. Grabbing Hyacinth around the waist, he ripped her back inside, and most of Mordecai along with her. Shifting to his brother's belt, he jerked him all the way inside, as the wolf slammed its snarling head into the crack.

Hyacinth and Lawrence and Caleb all pressed as far back against each other as was possible inside the hollow tree.

Mordecai slumped down into the bottom of the hole, curling up on their feet, instantly asleep.

The wolf raged and snapped, slavering, spilling its wet anger all over Mordecai's rounded back.

The crack was still closing.

"Best withdraw," Caleb said quietly. "Or you'll lose that fine shaggy head."

The wolf retreated slowly until it was only a sniffling nose and dripping tongue and bared front fangs.

The crack closed.

Mordecai muttered something in his sleep and shifted awkwardly against Hyacinth's shins, hooking his arm around her ankles.

From above, faint orange light found its way dimly down the hollow tree.

Eight inches away, Caleb managed to shift and face her.

"What was the point of that?" he asked.

"What was the point?" Hyacinth sputtered. She felt her adrenaline turning to anger. "The point is that we are alive. That's the point!"

The orange light above them vanished. Warm, moist, rotten darkness swallowed them whole.

"Hy," Lawrence said quietly. "Are we stuck?"

EIGHT

NIMIANE HELD THE CAT tight, stroking her blood-sticky fur, feeling the low, angry drumming of her inner purr.

She faced the healed tree, a cedar as mighty as any she had ever seen. A cedar that had swallowed children and had then sent up new branches as thick as galley masts, and had splintered stone beneath Nimiane's feet with deep, worming roots.

Her men were all around, shifting quietly in the darkness, now that the fire arches had dwindled, waiting for a command from Nimroth's ancient daughter. Every drop of Nimiane's blackened blood itched in her veins, hot with anger. It would have burned its way out of a lesser body, but she had mastered the struggle of immortality long ago, when she had imprisoned her raving father and taken his many thrones.

"Queen." The wizard who spoke was young and vain, still struggling to grow his downy blond beard. She listened to him throw back his cape and bow, but she did not look his way. "If you would allow us to burn the tree, or even set to it with axes, this could be ended quickly. We could fetch you this green man, kill the others, and be done."

Nimiane extended her hand toward the wizard's voice and beckoned him. His steps were hesitant as he approached, but no man here would ever defy her. When she felt the warmth of his life beside her, she let her fingertips gently find his face, his lips. And then she wormed a whisper into the young man's mind.

Fool.

She drew his life into her as easily as breathing. His heat vanished, and then his breath. And last, his terrified thoughts. The man's body, dry and ashen, collapsed beside her, brittle and rustling like leaves.

He had not been strong. Consuming him had been as satisfying as dipping her tongue in water when she had a thirst large enough for rivers. But it had been calming nonetheless.

Nimiane could have split the tree with one finger. She could have burned it with a word. But she didn't need to. She knew there were no human lives inside it. There were no souls she could touch with her own. And the only trace of the young green man was on the ground at her feet, where vines lay coiled with trampled grapes.

The children were gone. And they had been by the time Bast had returned to her and she had found her way to the scene of the struggle.

Strangest of all, they were gone without any trace of magic. No spells tainted the air with their acidic taste. No ghostly vine fire had left trails on the tree.

She had waited. She had been patient. And still, she could sense no lives within.

HYACINTH WAS DREAMING. SHE was dreaming that she was trapped inside a tree, balled up in the bottom of a hole with Lawrence sweating on top of her, unable to straighten her legs, raise her arms.

She was barely able to breathe.

"Wake up." Someone was grabbing her shoulder.

Hyacinth jerked, trying to slap the hand away. But her right arm was pinned to her side, and Lawrence's legs were on top of her left.

She was in fact balled up in the bottom of a hole inside a tree. Lawrence was practically sitting on her lap, and Caleb's rounded back was crushing her.

Mordecai was the only one standing and awake. Daylight and a tiny trace of coolness trickled down the hollow trunk above him. He was the one who had grabbed her shoulder.

"You're all right," Mordecai said. "It was just a dream."

Hyacinth sniffed at the stagnant air, thick with hours of breath and sweat, and already rotten to start.

"No," she said. "It wasn't a dream. What was I doing?"

"Kicking and shouting," Mordecai said. "Here, stand up. Get some blood in your legs."

With his one good arm, he lifted Lawrence's legs off of her, and he used his foot to push Caleb's back a few inches farther away. Then he extended his hand to Hyacinth.

Hyacinth grunted and tried to get her bare feet underneath her, but they were numb and clumsy. After a moment of trying to do it herself, she grabbed Mordecai's forearm.

He pulled her up and she immediately slumped back against the rotten wood wall, grimacing as a roar of needles marched through her feet.

Sore didn't even begin to describe how Hyacinth felt. Her joints felt like unpopped knuckles. Her skull was trying to expand and contract like a bone lung. Her spine was refusing to straighten, her right shoulder felt like it was stuck in her ear, and her bare feet seemed to be made of bruises. She watched Mordecai slowly roll his damaged shoulder. The fungal teeth created rolling hills beneath his shirt.

"You okay?" Hyacinth asked.

Mordecai nodded, looking up the tree at the small patch of daylight at least a dozen feet above them. "Better than I could be," he said. "Although I am incredibly hungry."

"Nothing I can do about that," Hyacinth said. "Sorry."

Mordecai looked at her, studying her face as if she was joking.

"You can open this tree up," he said. "If the witch was going to burn it or peel it open, she would have done it by now. And to be honest, I don't know why she didn't."

Hyacinth looked around at the rough cedar walls. The tree seemed a great deal healthier than it had been the night before. Outside, she would expect new branches. And if she had the energy to really feel for them, she wouldn't have been surprised by root fingers hundreds of feet long.

"You want me to crack the tree open?" She blinked and rubbed her eyes. That was different from prodding growth. That was destruction and decay. She wasn't sure she could do that.

"I don't just want you to," Mordecai said. "You must. Otherwise, you've crafted a rather large coffin for four."

Hyacinth rubbed her eyes and tried to think.

"Can't you pull it open with vines?"

Mordecai laughed.

"I don't know what magic you used or how you shut us in here—"

"No magic," Hyacinth said. "I told you that already. And I didn't do this. I just asked the tree to do it."

"—and I don't care right now," Mordecai continued. "But if you want us to live, you will get started on the counterspell really soon."

Hyacinth brushed back her hair and didn't try to hide the anger in her eyes. "No spells. I just asked. That's it."

"Then ask again," Mordecai said.

"I'd be asking the tree to harm itself," Hyacinth said. "I've never done that. It feels wrong. And I don't know if it will work. You have a knife, right? Can't you carve a door?"

"Maybe. But not before our brothers wake up and need to relieve themselves."

"Relieve themselves?" Hyacinth asked. "What do you . . . oh."

Mordecai shifted his weight from side to side. "I'm not just hungry," he said. "I really have to go."

And as soon as he said it, she did too.

"Right. Okay." Hyacinth faced the soft cedar wall and ran her palms across it.

"You're not really asking it to harm itself," Mordecai said. "It can grow together again after. And won't it be healthier with us gone?"

Hyacinth nodded. He wasn't wrong. And she wasn't wrong to ask the tree to split its own gut wide open.

"I feel like Jonah," Mordecai said. "Waiting to be vomited up by the fish."

"You know about Jonah?" Hyacinth asked, but her senses were already too focused on the tree to listen to the answer.

"Here," she whispered, and she dragged her thumbnail

slowly up as high as she could reach, leaving a faint groove carved in the soft wood. "Or wherever is easiest. Please."

Nothing.

"You don't want us in here," she whispered. "Not really."

Hyacinth summoned up every memory of wood splitting, every image of a cracked tree, along with thoughts of survival and release and escape.

The wood was alive and thriving under her touch, strong and vibrant. She could tell that the tree was feeling wind and basking in sun, but she felt no response to her suggestions at all. Not even rejection.

"What does it want with us?" Mordecai asked. "Can't you reason with it?"

"It isn't like that," Hyacinth said. "It's not an animal. Trees are more like living books, libraries of lives and times. I'm just someone who likes the books, even though I can't really read them. They can be angry like a storm or at peace in the breeze, but it's not like they have goals."

"How do you know?" Mordecai asked.

Hyacinth was silent. She didn't know. She just felt. But, of course, she could be wrong. She hadn't made the trees or taught them how to wrap their years in rings. All she'd ever really been able to do was get things to grow quickly.

"Do what you like." Mordecai pressed himself back against the wood wall and looked up at the light. "But I think you should stop asking politely and command this thing in the name of God and all His angels to let us out right now."

Hyacinth tried again. She shut her eyes and pressed her head against the wood between her hands. The stuffy smell faded. If Mordecai was talking, she didn't hear him. She even forgot the feeling of the wood against her skin.

She sensed only the tree. Strength. Glory. Age. Pride. Thousands of trees had come from this one. Entire civilizations of cardinals had nested in its branches, and a record of every song sung and egg hatched and nest raided was written in the rings. In the rings, those birds still sang. . . .

Hyacinth began to write a story. She whispered it into the wood and heard it echo back in the grain.

Shame. Shame for the tree that devoured a green man . . . boy . . . and a healing grower. Shame for the tree defiled with human meat rotting in its belly. Its branches hold only vultures and their spew, and its wood will grace no halls and hear no laughter. That tree is less than rot.

The trunk shook, and Hyacinth felt the cedar's anger.

A split opened beneath her face, but she didn't open her eyes and she didn't stop the flood of her thoughts. Not until she felt warm air blowing on her face and Mordecai's hand on her shoulder.

Hyacinth opened her eyes. Her chest was at ground level and she was looking at rippling green grass climbing a symmetrical mound the size of an enormous barn.

There were other trees as well, surrounding the mound in an extended ring, and between each pair of trees there stood carved white stones, heavy with moss.

"This isn't California," Hyacinth said.

"What did you do?" Mordecai asked. "No . . . don't," he added quickly. "You didn't *do* anything."

He helped Hyacinth up and out onto the grass before climbing out after her.

The grass felt lovely beneath Hyacinth's bare feet, spongy turf with lush green blades, cool and moist. The mound inside the circle of trees had clearly been constructed by someone, just as the stones had been placed and the trees planted.

Mordecai was moving away quickly, toward the next tree in the ring.

"Where are you going?" Hyacinth asked.

"Don't ask," he said. And then he stepped out of view.

Hyacinth, wondering if she might be able to find a spot with a bit more privacy, turned her attention back to the tree.

Apart from being a cedar, it looked nothing like the tree they had entered in the lightning tree grove. And the crack in the trunk was only a few inches wide.

"Oh, no!" Hyacinth dropped onto her knees. "Lawrence!" She tore grass away from the trunk and shoved both hands into the crack, prepared to soundly curse the tree, to curse it until it welcomed her back inside or spat out her brother.

Her hands vanished completely into the trunk. Shocked, she jerked them out and waited a moment for her heart to settle back down. Then, spreading her hands wide, she leaned her head toward the crack.

The smell of sweaty boys and dirt greeted her. Caleb was on his feet, right at her eye level, looking frightened and with his knife already drawn. Lawrence was blinking at the bottom of the hole.

"Hy?" he asked. "Are they gone? Can we get out now?"

"Go!" Mordecai shouted.

Hyacinth pulled her head back out of the tree. Mordecai was sprinting toward her as two men entered the circle, with wide-bladed swords already drawn, spitting anger in a language Hyacinth had never heard before. The men were led by a pair of enormously shaggy orange dogs, bounding through the grass in front of them.

Hyacinth slid feetfirst back into the tree and waited, with her palms against the wood.

She didn't have to wait long.

Mordecai slammed into Caleb and then sat on Lawrence. While the boys yelped, Hyacinth gave the tree a single word.

Close.

And the tree responded immediately.

This time no snapping wolf risked its head. The trunk closed, and Mordecai and Hyacinth looked at each other.

Mordecai smiled. "I think I just desecrated their sacred grove."

Lawrence scrambled up onto his feet, squeezing a space for himself between the brothers.

"Hy," he said, "I really have to go to the bathroom."

Hyacinth sighed.

Mordecai almost laughed. "Give it a minute. Then open the tree again."

"What's going on?" Caleb asked. "Is the witch still out there? I waited all night for her to carve it open."

Hyacinth shut her eyes. Her mind was struggling to understand what had just happened. Maybe Mordecai could laugh about it, but her stomach was binding itself into a lump that was part lead and part panic.

How could they not be in California?

Or maybe they were in California right now, while they were inside the tree, but they weren't once they went outside. Maybe she'd opened the crack wrong. Maybe she needed to open a different part of the trunk, or start with a different ring. But she hadn't done it; the tree had. . . .

She could feel her breath quickening, and even with her eyes shut, the space felt tighter than it had all night with three boys, damp with sweat, snoring around her. She was the one damp with sweat now. Her forehead was slick with a cold layer, and a single droplet rolled down her spine.

What had she done? Her ribs shook. But just once. She managed to bite back the sob. That was the fear. And fear wasn't helpful right now.

Fear that she would never find their way back. Fear that her parents would return to a home without her and without her brother. Instead they would be devoured by a witch with mushroom men and a creepy cat.

She bit her lip harder, hard enough to turn her fear into anger. Hard enough to draw blood.

That's not how this was going to go. She would find her way home, and the witch was going to die.

"We have to figure this out," she said quietly. "We will figure this out."

"What?" Lawrence asked. "Figure what out, Hy?" He shuffled in place. "I really have to go."

"Mordecai," Caleb whispered. "What did she do?"

Gritting her teeth and closing her eyes, Hyacinth tried not to listen. Facing the back of the hollow, across from the first crack, she tried to clear her mind and focus on where she wanted to be. Somewhere the witch wasn't. Somewhere safe. Somewhere they wouldn't die.

"She opened a way," Mordecai said. "I think the old woman collected dead lightning trees for a reason."

Not dead, Hyacinth thought. She touched her bitten lip and then touched the wood. *Somewhere with my family. Somewhere near this blood.*

This time the tree did not need waking. The life in

the grain had already quickened. The trunk shivered and groaned all around them. Rocks bounced and hopped beneath their feet, and the hollow inside the tree began to close from the bottom up.

Lawrence jumped, trying to grab on to the sides, but he only managed to throw his arms around Hyacinth's neck. They slammed into Mordecai and Caleb, and all four of them writhed and climbed, pulling up their feet as quickly as they could while the wood rumbled shut.

"Stop!" Hyacinth yelled. "Please!"

The sides began to close in.

But they weren't just closing in. They were becoming smooth. The bottom stopped rising and flattened. Above them, the chimney hollow rumbled shut, cutting off the light.

All four sides pressed in tight against them and then stopped. Lawrence was wriggling against Hyacinth's side, and one of the brothers was breathing on her face. The ceiling was less than a foot above their heads.

The smell of burned wood was even more powerful than the smell of breath.

"Hyacinth," Mordecai said simply. "This is worse."

"Shush," Hyacinth said. "I hear voices."

She pressed her ear against the wall beside her. But instead of listening, she felt the wood lurch stiffly. A seam of light opened all the way up the center, and a slice of cool air found Hyacinth's face.

The voices grew louder.

"It's a door?" Caleb asked. "Push it open."

"Hy," Lawrence said, and she could hear the urgency in his voice.

"I know," she whispered. "You have to go. Just hold on a second."

Leaning forward, careful not to rest her weight on the doorway, Hyacinth put her left eye to the crack.

The room was octagonal, lit with oversize lightbulbs hanging from heavy chains from a high beamed ceiling. The walls were made of smooth stone, and they were lined with loose doors and cabinets and boxes.

In the center of the room, there was huge plank table with six people around it. On the side facing Hyacinth, two men and one woman were examining picture frames— crudely constructed and occasionally charred. The man in the center had dark hair, and even though he seemed young, his face looked like it had been made from a saddle and sandpaper, and his eyes were set in deep shadow beneath his brows. He was wearing a tan linen shirt with an over-both-shoulders double holster that held a gun beneath each arm.

The other two—a round man with a long beard, and an old redheaded woman with a face made of freckles— were more distracted by the frames and much softer.

The hard young man leaned back in his chair and focused his attention on three people sitting quite still across from him—also two men and one woman.

Their backs were to Hyacinth, but she knew them.

The Viking.

And her parents.

TRUDIE HATED THE ROOM. The Room of Ways, they had been told it was called. Why they had to give their statements in front of strange paintings and carved cabinets and ancient doors, she did not know. Even worse, there were two coffins in the room as well—three if she counted the Egyptian sarcophagus that had been converted into something that looked more like a wardrobe. She had given it no more than a glance—enough to see that the ancient rituals depicted all over it focused on honoring Reshep, the god of lightning, war, and pestilence. A real charmer.

She slipped her hand off the arm of her chair and slid it under her husband's on his.

"Do you need to take a break, Mrs. Smith?" The boy with the guns spoke with a twang. She had last seen him when he was barely ten. Bobby Boone, all jokes and smiles. Now, even as young as he still was, he would have been intimidating among any group of killers. Of course, that was probably the point. That's why the Order had selected him for the job he now held. Like a sheriff in the Old West . . . he was the lawdog, investigator of violent threats against members. Blood Avenger when lives were lost. His title was Avengel.

"No, sir, I'm fine." She smiled. "And please call me Trudie."

"Yes, ma'am," he said, smiling. "And I'd appreciate it if you would just call me Robert. Or Bobby, like you used to."

"Well, Bobby," Albert said, "we've brought you some samples of the frames. We've given you a full and complete description of the creature we killed. Is there anything else you need from us before we leave?"

Bobby Boone tapped the table, and for a moment he watched the bearded man and the redheaded woman as they examined every millimeter of the frames.

"This woman," he said. "Granlea Quarles. You believe that she has been intentionally gathering and milling lightning trees for use in way-making spells."

Albert nodded. "Although I suspect she is only attempting to continue old Isaac's work. And now that the property is ours, we will be erasing every trace of their efforts."

The young man studied Albert, unblinking. Trudie felt her husband's grip tighten. She heard him swallow.

"Excuse me," Trudie said. "Robert." She smiled quickly. "It's hard to call you Bobby now. But I hope you don't mind if I ask you a personal question."

Trudie could feel Albert tensing up even more. He had no idea what she was doing. They had discussed their plan—get in, say as little as possible, get out, get home.

"Ma'am." Bobby grinned. "You can get as personal as you like. I hope I haven't done something wrong."

"Oh, no," Trudie said. "And if you had, I'd let your mama handle it." She was letting a little bit of drawl creep into her own voice now. If she had some sweet tea, she would have handed him a glass. She wanted the tone in the room to change. She needed him to look at her and see his mama's old friend, and feel himself being put just a little bit on trial. "You look like you've been through a lot. And it's not just that you're all grown up. You look, well, you look like you've been through a war."

Bobby Boone's smile faded a little. "You could say that, ma'am." He straightened up in his chair. "I'm young—too young for the Avengel's job, more than likely. But I've been living dog years for a while now—seven years in every one. And I expect it will feel like that from here until the end."

The pair that had been inspecting the frames stacked them all neatly on the table, apparently finished with their task, and then turned to leave.

"Nothing," the bearded man said.

"Lightning force," the woman added. "And lots of it. But no way-magic at all. No manipulation of the grain."

Robert Boone nodded, and the two exited the room through a heavy iron door, whispering as they went, but then slamming it behind them.

"All right, then," Robert said. "You've asked a personal question. Now I'll ask you one, Mrs. Smith. How many children do you have?"

Trudie's throat cinched tight.

"I'm sorry." Thor leaned forward, placing his big hands on the table. "Could the two of you catch up at some other time? You know the family, Boone. And you have whatever records you might need. Albert and Trudie have fulfilled every duty as members and more. And I've donated the use of my plane. Unfortunately, I need to be on my way."

"And I thank you for that," Robert said. "But I do have a point, Mr. Smith." He pointed at Albert. "You believe that a crazy old woman successfully opened a way between worlds, allowing four monstrous creatures to enter, but you still trust her enough to leave her in possession of your children?"

"Of course not," Albert said. "I don't trust her at all."

Thor rapped his knuckles on the table. "On the way here, I delivered his children to Llewelyn's camp up north, along with my own godson."

HYACINTH BARELY MANAGED to turn around in the tight box.

"Are you sure the back is closed?" she whispered. "We can't go out this way. Not right now."

"Of course we're sure," Caleb said. "We wouldn't be in here at all if the back were open."

"It wouldn't be the back if it were open," Mordecai muttered.

"Hyacinth," Lawrence whined. "I'm going to have an accident."

"Just . . . okay." Hyacinth spread her hands against the sides. "Hold on, L. Just hold on."

But Lawrence tried to wriggle past her.

"No," she hissed, and blocked him. "You can't!"

"Yes," Lawrence said. "I can."

Caleb and Mordecai tried to grab on to him, but he was already in motion. Lunging forward, Lawrence put his shoulder into Hyacinth's stomach, yelled, and drove her out through the doors, tumbling with her onto cold stone.

Hyacinth landed hard, and her breath escaped on impact. She heard her mother scream as Lawrence rolled right over her and jumped to his feet.

There was a man standing up with two guns drawn, pointing at her, at Lawrence, and then back at Mordecai and Caleb as they stepped out of what had apparently once been an Egyptian sarcophagus.

"I really need a bathroom," Lawrence said, dancing in place. "Super bad."

NINE

GRANLEA QUARLES OPENED HER eyes for the first time in hours. Her arms and legs were spread wide and she was flat on her back . . . on the ceiling.

She was in her living room, looking down past tendrils of her dangling white hair at the wreckage on the floor and at the witch, rocking slowly in her rocking chair, stroking a bloody white cat.

The pressure pinning her to the ceiling was immense, and it pushed against every inch of her body. Even breathing was difficult.

Before falling unconscious, she had witnessed the arrival of the witch's wolves and hunters and wizards. She had seen them stream in through the open doorway in her wall and march away with confidence.

"How," Granlea gasped, "did it go?"

The witch didn't look up, but her hand paused for a moment on her cat.

"You know," Granlea said, "I bear you no ill will."

The cat slowly looked up, directly into Granlea's eyes.

And what Granlea saw was anger. Hunger. But above all else, cruelty.

"When my brother, Isaac, began ..." She paused, fighting for a large-enough breath to finish her sentence. "When Isaac began his quest, he was seeking faeries."

"Faeren," the witch snarled, and then spat on the floor.

"But he thought faeries were creatures," Granlea breathed heavily. "Grand like you."

"Fool," the witch said. "I know your Isaac. He wandered into Endor, clothed all in white, claiming to be an ambassador from the children of men. When my servants brought him to me, he begged to be made undying and trained in Endorian power. In exchange, he offered me his world." The witch coughed, scraping a laugh up her throat. "I offered to apprentice him to my own father, Nimroth Blackstar, and your Isaac wept with joy."

"What did you do?" Granlea asked.

The cat blinked.

"I kept my word," the witch said. "I presented him as a gift to my mad father. And he was consumed."

"You sent him to his death?" Granlea asked.

"He is not dead. His soul has fed the Blackstar. He will live on forever, wherever one of our blood may strike. He is as undying as the incubi bound up in my veins."

Granlea shut her eyes, and the pressure on her body almost erased her consciousness again.

"Will you also try to barter?" The witch laughed.

"What have you to offer me? There are only two things I desire. Verily, three that will sate me. Four that can bring me happiness."

The rocking chair sighed, and Granlea reopened her eyes. The witch was on her feet. She and the cat both turned their faces up toward the woman on the ceiling. The cat's eyes were locked onto Granlea's, but the witch's gaze was as blind as it was beautiful.

"Four things," Granlea said, panting. "I'm sure I can help you with one of them."

"I desire the rule of this and every other world, the taste of every living thing upon my tongue. Can you bend me every knee?"

Granlea tried to shake her head, but her dangling hair barely wavered.

"No," the witch said. "Now look on me as I am."

In a flash, the beautiful witch-queen was gone, and in her place, there stood a woman as shriveled and bald as a diseased monkey. Dark pus dripped from open sores on her arms and legs. Her patchy scalp was covered with bloody scratches, scabbed black, and her lips were split and torn. She had no eyes. She had only oozing scratches and claw marks striping down her brows, across her baggy, empty eyelids, and down her cheeks.

In her skeletal arms, she still held her cat. And the cat's eyes still searched Granlea's.

"Can you heal my eyes?" the witch snarled. "Can you

give me sight that is again my own? Can you ease the burning in my veins?"

Granlea gasped in disgust. She wanted to turn her head and look away, but she couldn't even manage to blink.

"No," the witch said. "The cursed man who took my eyes has only two more living sons, and they have dared defy me. Can you gift me the sons of the eye-thief? Can you stretch them on an altar and plunge a knife into their hearts? Can you fill a bowl with their blood so I might dip my cat's tongue and quench my hate?"

The wrinkled witch hissed up at Granlea, and then spat on the floor between her own feet.

"No," the witch said. "These things I will do for myself, and owe you nothing."

In another flash, the witch transformed back into her former beauty, then sat back down in the rocking chair.

"There are one thousand lightning-struck trees in your grove," the witch said. "Four hundred and forty-four more twice struck. It is a powerful number. The sons of the eye-thief opened a way through one of them, but those mongrel boys may return through any of the others. Even now my way rites are being prepared, and the bloods will soon be mixed. I will open every way, I will set in every tree a crossroads, and all will lead to me." The cat began to clean the witch's arm with its tongue.

"Why keep me up here?" Granlea asked. "Why not just kill me?"

"You are the mistress of the trees," the witch said. "Your blood will be required." She sighed, rocking gently in the chair, staring blankly at the empty fireplace.

"In this place, I shall open the greatest Grove of Ways since Semiramis fled the wind-hung gardens of Babylon, since Fuhi gathered the beasts with his gopherwood doors. I will be the mistress of worlds."

"*Blind* mistress," Granlea grunted. "Too bad you won't see them."

Hyacinth watched Lawrence run for the big iron door while Robert Boone rose to his feet, drew both guns, and tracked him.

"Stay put, kid," Boone said. But Lawrence kept running.

"Lawrence!" Trudie yelled.

"Hi, Mom," Lawrence said. "I'll be right back. I have to find a bathroom."

"No," said Boone. "You don't."

A fiery band of light erupted out of the sarcophagus, winding around Robert Boone's arms and slamming him down into his chair so hard that it tipped over backward.

Albert and Thor jumped out of their seats, and Trudie clamped a hand over a scream.

Mordecai and Caleb stepped into the room.

Lawrence managed to tug open the iron door, dancing while he did it.

"Down the hall to the right," Thor said.

"And then come right back," Albert added.

Lawrence slid out into the hall and sprinted out of view.

"First, Hyacinth Smith arrives," Robert Boone drawled from his back. "The shameful young witch, long hidden away by her parents."

"She's not a witch," Mordecai said, and he jerked his burning hand, flipping Robert's chair upright so hard that it nearly slammed his face into the table before the vines held it tight.

"Then I expect you're not a wizard either."

"No, sir," Mordecai said. "Wizards are useless."

"Then explain to me," Robert said, "how you reopened and entered a sealed and forbidden doorway that is kept in a room that has for centuries prevented all such travel."

"He doesn't have to explain anything to you," Caleb said. "And the only witch we care about is the one we plan to kill."

"Or die trying," Mordecai said.

Trudie slipped down out of her chair and helped her daughter onto her feet.

"Hy, love, what's going on?" she asked, brushing Hyacinth's hair out of her face. "How is this possible? What happened?"

"We came through the trees," Hyacinth said. "More of those mushroom monsters came. They all answer to this awful witch, and we hid in a hollow tree."

"And who are these boys?" Albert asked.

"Caleb and Mordecai Westmore," Hyacinth said. Both brothers lowered their heads toward her father in acknowledgment. "The sixth and seventh sons of Amram Iothric. They came through one of Granlea's frames, and the monsters followed. The witch came through last night, trying to find them."

"Who is this witch?" Robert Boone pushed back hard, until he had forced his chair to rest flat on the floor. "Name her."

Hyacinth looked from Mordecai to Caleb. She could see that neither of them had any interest in sharing details of their conflict with strangers, even one that they had already restrained.

"Tell him," Hyacinth said. "And untie him."

Mordecai and Caleb both hesitated. Thor drew a long knife from his belt and strode around the table to begin cutting vines. As he did, Hyacinth heard him whisper in the young man's ear, "No guns, Robert. You hear me?"

Robert Boone's face gave absolutely no sign that he had heard anything at all.

Mordecai slumped into an empty chair, and the vines all fell slack before Thor managed to get his blade through a single one.

"Nimiane," Caleb said. "Witch-queen of Endor, daughter of Nimroth Blackstar."

Robert Boone tore his arms loose, pulled his knees up

through the vines, hopped onto the seat of his chair, and then over the back and onto the floor. Both guns still dangled in his hands.

"Nimroth," he drawled. "That's a name I've seen in the old rolls, but his stories are lost in myth. There has been no trace of him for centuries. And Nimiane is only present in a few old poems—the beautiful devourer of men and wizards." He studied the brothers for a moment. "You have faced the Blackstar? You have seen Nimroth?"

"No," Mordecai said. "We have not. Nimiane overthrew him. Our father faced her, and although he took the eyes from her skull, he was thrown down and destroyed. We have faced her and failed. We faced her again, and instead of fighting to an end, as I had intended, Hyacinth Smith brought us here."

"I didn't mean to," Hyacinth said.

"Yes, you did," Mordecai said. "You begged the wood to open a way to your mother and father. And here we are."

"Witchcraft," Robert Boone said. "I'm sorry, but there's no other word for it."

"Hush, Robert," Thor said. "Do not miss the forest for the trees. These children are allies."

"I only asked the tree," Hyacinth said. "The wood was already connected, the rings are all part of one great tale, and they touch each other in ways I never imagined before yesterday."

"If I hadn't seen you fall out of Reshep's box, I would

call you a lunatic," Robert drawled. Then he focused on Mordecai. "If this Nimiane shares the Blackstar blood, then she is undying. She cannot be killed, but she can be bound and buried. We will be your allies in this fight, but you must submit yourself to our governance and abide by our laws. There will be no magic. If you are found to have conducted, performed, or conjured any spell, you will be subject to the Order's judgment, up to and including death."

Mordecai laughed out loud, but Robert Boone was perfectly serious. He faced Hyacinth.

"Hyacinth Smith, this applies to you already. And by your own testimony, you have opened and passed through ways, which is strictly forbidden in this Order and has been for centuries."

"You can't be serious," Albert said. He pulled his daughter away from her mother and tucked her under his arm. "She has a touch, a green touch beyond what is normal, yes, but what good do threats do?"

"Mr. Smith." Robert shook his head. "I am not making any threat. It is a simple description of the Order's position on such things. You have hidden her and kept her off the official rolls, but she is no secret, and neither is her gift. Oak groves sprouting up overnight might be overlooked, but the creation of ways is, and always has been, forbidden. It is the magic of faeren and imps and lesser demons, and it opens, quite literally, whole worlds of deadly and uncontrollable trouble." He laughed and gestured at the vines, and then at the brothers. "Has this not been thoroughly demonstrated by the presence and recent adventures of those four who just tumbled into this room? A foolish old woman has already opened ways for a witch-queen as old as King Arthur, and as many monsters as she might choose to bring. If this girl, your daughter, cannot control her gift, then she is more dangerous to us all, not less. I have sworn to uphold the laws of this Order, sir, to the point of my death. I am bound by my vows. Way-magic cannot be tolerated, nor can its practitioners, intentional or otherwise."

For a long moment the room was silent. And then Thor scratched his beard, the thick red hair crackling like a campfire in the stillness.

"Bobby," Trudie said. "Please."

Lawrence slipped back inside the iron door and banged it shut behind him, grinning.

"That was a close one," he said. He jogged around the table to his mother, throwing his arms around her before studying the room for the first time. His smile vanished.

"Where are we?" he asked. "What's going on?"

"I think it's time we took this discussion elsewhere," Robert said. "I'd appreciate it if you all would be so kind as to follow me."

"Son," Thor said, "I think you're making a mistake."

"It is mine to make, sir."

"Maybe," Thor said. "But could we discuss it in the hall? A private word might be in order."

Robert Boone paused, surprised.

"You may be the Order's brute enforcer at the moment," Thor said. "But there are others in this place who contribute wisdom. And experience."

Not waiting for an answer, the Viking opened the door.

"Albert, Gertrude, would you be willing to join us in the hallway?"

Albert bent down, kissing his daughter on the head, and then whispered in her ear, "Get them out of here. However you did it, do it again. You aren't safe here. Not at all."

"But the house," Hyacinth said. "If we go back . . ."

"Don't," her father whispered. "That place will be swarming soon. Somewhere else. Somewhere safe."

"Albert," Thor said again. "Please."

Albert nodded and released his daughter, but Trudie immediately threw her arms around her.

"You're my perfect flower," she whispered. "Hide. But find us soon. Be safe."

Hyacinth didn't understand what was happening as her mother pulled away and both her parents moved toward the door.

"Lawrence," Albert said. "Perhaps you'd better stay with us for a minute."

Hyacinth watched her confused brother trail after her father.

Thor held the door open as Albert and Trudie and Lawrence stepped out into the hall. As the door began to close behind them, Lawrence met his sister's stare, and his eyes were full of fear.

"Why isn't Hy coming?" he asked.

"I know what you're doing," Robert said.

"You don't know anything," Thor replied. And the door banged shut.

Instantly, Caleb jumped forward and slid two heavy iron dead bolts into the stone wall, sealing them in.

Hyacinth swallowed hard, and it hurt when she did. What had just happened? Blinking quickly, trying to ignore her hot blurring eyes, she focused on the table in front of her.

"I'm sorry," Mordecai said softly. "I am so sorry."

"Sorry for what?" Caleb asked. "We have to move quickly, Hy. Now. We have to get out of here."

"You're not my brother," Hyacinth said. "You don't get to call me that."

"Okay . . ." Caleb looked at Mordecai for help. "I'll call you whatever you like. But we need to open one of these doorways and leave. The iron door is strong, but it won't hold out for long against serious effort."

Hyacinth walked to her father's empty chair and sat down. She had no one. No brothers and no sisters. No parents. She couldn't go where they could go. She couldn't be what they could be.

"Hyacinth?" Caleb asked. "Miss Smith? We need to hurry."

"There's nowhere I want to go," Hyacinth said. "I can't go home. I only just got one, and now it's gone. All I wanted to do was find my parents. I thought if I found them, we'd be safe. It would all be fine. We could stay with them." She crossed her arms on the table and slumped her head onto them. She didn't want to cry. She wouldn't let herself. She would just sit in the strange cold room until she was numb.

"But there are lots of places to go," Caleb said. "This room is full of doors. And the lightning tree frames are still on the table."

"I'm not your taxi," Hyacinth said.

"I don't know what that is."

"It doesn't matter." Hyacinth exhaled slowly, forcing herself to breathe evenly. "I can't open a doorway and definitely not a frame. I woke a tree, and I'm not sure I even did that."

Hyacinth heard the chair scrape beside her, and Mordecai sat down.

"Your father has faith in you," Mordecai said quietly. "More faith in you than he has in himself."

Hyacinth didn't answer.

"It is hard when those we want to protect us no longer

can. When they look to us to protect them. Do you know the story of Moses?"

Hyacinth sat up and stared at the beamed ceiling high above her. "What does Moses have to do with anything?" she asked.

"When the sun god sent his soldiers to slaughter the newborn children of the Ram, Moses's mother made a boat of a basket and floated her baby away on the river."

"And?" Hyacinth asked.

"She could not save her son and keep him. And if she kept him, her son would never save her."

Hyacinth turned in her seat, looking in Mordecai's eyes. They were as gray as distant storms in morning. And they looked every bit as wet as Hyacinth's felt. He wasn't just talking about her.

"You are in the basket now, Hyacinth Smith." He smiled. "And so are we. They have floated us away. Now let us save them all."

Caleb laughed.

Hyacinth blinked and tried to smile.

"It sounds good. But I don't know what that means."

"That man may have heard of the Blackstar and Endorian blood, but he has no true taste for what a devourer it is. Nimiane has turned cities to ash with only her thirst and has driven armies mad with nightmare. Her breath is death, her blood runs thick with demons, and to be killed by her is no escape—she crafts chains, even for ghosts. If simple men with weapons are sent to face her, they will all be devoured. She has a door into this world now, and she will make it hers."

The iron door rattled, and a fist drummed on the outside.

Mordecai held out his hand, and Hyacinth watched the small ghost of vine fire twist on his palm. Cautiously at first, she reached out her hand, and then covered his palm with her own.

"Let us end her," Mordecai said. "There is no one who can protect us. So let us be the protectors."

"But she can't die," Hyacinth said, staring down at her hand on his. "You said that."

"You heard that man." Mordecai grinned. "Even undead, she can be bound and buried. She did it to her father. Let her live on, but as he does—mad and in chains."

A voice shouted an order in the hall, and then the chamber boomed with a heavy impact. Dust rained down around the iron door.

"Right now," Caleb said, "we just need an exit."

Hyacinth stood up and scanned the various doorways that lined the walls. "But where will we go?" she asked.

Mordecai released her hand and stood up beside her. "First, somewhere safe. From there, we hurdle teeth and slide into the monster's belly."

TEN

SQUID LAY PANTING IN the shade beside the trunk of a redwood tree. He had not killed the cat, but he had tasted it. And it had tasted evil.

His teeth had penetrated the enemy's haunches, but not nearly as deeply as the wolf's teeth had penetrated Squid's.

Squid felt pain, because he had been bitten badly and his right rear leg was useless to him for the time being and perhaps forever. He felt pride, because his pack humans had escaped and two of the wolves had been killed. He felt loss, because Shark and Ray were no more. They had been valiant, as all dogs should be. But the final wolf, the wolf that still paced the lightning grove, the wolf that Squid always kept upwind, that wolf had broken the necks of bold Shark and bold Ray, and had then torn them open.

Squid felt loneliness, because all around, he saw only enemies.

The wind was changing, and he rose onto three legs and hobbled in the direction it was blowing. The wind must touch the wolf first. If it touched Squid first, then it would carry his scent to the wolf and the wolf would come and the wolf would break his neck and tear him open.

Slumping down into new shade, Squid also felt hunger. And thirst. But he forgot them both, because the wind was carrying new smells. He lifted his nose and cocked his ears and sniffed at the air until he saw the smells clearly in his mind.

There were many of the moving mushrooms. There were many unwashed men who smelled of fire and lizard dust. There was the wolf. There was very much blood. Very much. And there were very many ravens.

Squid felt drool beginning to pool in his lower jaw. More ravens than he had ever smelled. Many ravens here, upwind beside the house, and many more coming. So many. Very near the blood.

And then the smells began to move, and Squid wormed his way deeper into his shadow beneath the tree.

Squid watched as the fire-smelling men walked between the trees. They held four burning sticks in their hands and carried fire in a cage upon their lower backs and blood in a bowl upon their lower fronts. Strangest of all, the men all wore ladders on their backs, above the caged fires, and on the ladders the many ravens were perched—twelve to a man. The birds should have been shrieking. They should have been flying from the smoke that rose up beneath their ladders. But they did not. They were silent and still, except for the turnings of their heads as the unwashed men walked beneath them and paused at every tree, drawing four smoking shapes upon each trunk, and touching each with a drop of blood.

Squid dozed as the men continued, tucking his nose beneath his leg to shield his senses from the smoke. When he woke, it was because a man was drawing shapes on the trunk above him. The man turned and moved away, and all twelve ravens riding on his ladder eyed the injured dog on the ground.

THE WITCH SAT PERFECTLY still in Granlea's rocking chair. The cat was no longer on her lap. She had sent her eyes outside to observe the movements of her witch-dogs among the trees.

Bast had climbed up onto the roof of the house, and from there, the witch could see perfectly. The force had been assembled, and in a matter of hours they had marched from her gardens into the little house and out into the grove.

One hundred and forty-four witch-dogs, carrying more than seventeen hundred silent ravens. One hundred mushroom hunters, still thin and undergrown, but deadly enough for her needs. And five hundred veteran blade slaves—men whose souls Nimiane had bound to dark weapons, which were in turn bound to her will. If the slaves laid down their weapons, they laid down their lives.

If they turned against her or against her will, the blades turned against them.

The trees had all been marked with doors, four apiece. Her forces had fully assembled—hunters, then blade slaves, then witch-dogs arrayed in wide ranks between the grove and the house.

Bast looked down over the hundreds of ravens and hundreds of men and saw that the hunt had been well prepared. From her chair inside, Nimiane saw as well, and her mouth grew slick with hunger. She would force the grains and rings of the trees to open—four doors to a tree. But she could not guide them. The trees would do that, revealing ways long forgotten and lost or never discovered. They would span worlds.

Nimiane would be mother to a great Grove of Ways. She would be mistress of 5,776 doors. And beyond one of them, she would find her prey. First, children. And then worlds.

It was a feat that would have been beyond the reach of her father, even at his zenith. It was a feat well beyond her own reach, were it not for the force of the thousands of lashes of lightning collected in the trees.

Even so, it would require every ounce of life she had within her and all that she could gather. She would be vulnerable for a time. But only a brief time. The risk was more than worth it. Who was there for her to fear?

Her army was waiting. Her eyes were waiting. Her grove was waiting, and somewhere, so was her prey.

Nimiane rose from her chair and turned slowly to face inland, aligning herself with the cat-seen vision in her mind.

With a long, slow breath, she gathered herself, dropping her deceptive beauty, becoming the shriveled eyeless crone lined with scabs and sores. She extended her bare bony arms and began to gather all that she could hold.

Above her, blinking slowly, pale and barely conscious from her loss of blood, Granlea Quarles watched from the ceiling.

The frames on the walls cracked and rotted dry, disintegrating into ash—all but the open doorway behind the witch.

Nimiane stretched her mind back into Endor, tapping into the stores of life collected in her gardens—the many executed slaves and conquered foes, the drained forests and grasslands. She filled herself until she could hold no more, until stolen life spilled out of her and washed across the floor, until planks cracked and groaned with the voices of ghosts, and dust raced like ten thousand aimless ants around her feet, possessed with the souls of ancient enemies.

And still Nimiane filled herself—until her skin was a rippling rotten sea and her back arched and her jaw fell open and her teeth spun in her spotted gums, until her joints unhinged and twisted with a noise like giants chewing, until she stood only on two quivering toes, until even those toes rose off the ground.

The floor whispered her crimes in all the tongues of men.

The dust cursed her.

Nimiane walked into the dark realm of madness and destruction, and she was almost unable to return.

But she did.

Nimiane's tongue curled and spiraled in her mouth. A thousand voices struggled in her throat. And she released her first blow.

The earth quaked and rolled. Cliff faces shed one thousand tons of stone into the sea. The house heaved.

Nimiane fell to her knees, grabbing at the ground, fighting to funnel the strength beneath her men and into the trees.

The skin on every fingertip split and peeled back from the bone. Her veins snapped and writhed, struggling to explode from her body, and still she fought.

She threw more strength into her struggle. Another blow. And another.

Exhausted, fractured, many miles past death had she been mortal, Nimiane collapsed, unable to feel her pain or even shiver in her exhaustion. The floor was silent; the voices were gone. The ghosts, the souls, the stolen lives, all were finally spent and gone.

Granlea Quarles fell from the ceiling, landing on the plank floor like a sack of mud.

Outside, the witch's magic found its many marks.

Squid woke suddenly in strange stillness. He sat up by his tree trunk and threw his ears forward, lifting his nose in the air and sniffing. Above the house, out over the sea, a storm the color of midnight was forming. In the house, out of sight and out of scent, there were many strange things, things that pricked up the pelt between Squid's shoulders and set a low growl working in his chest without permission. In front of the house, an army was pressed into dense ranks, and thousands of black feathers fluttered in advance of the storm.

The first surge of life pulsed through him and into the tree before the ground even had a chance to tremor.

And then the trees shook. Rocks hopped. The army slipped and staggered, and the ravens—as one—cried out in piercing anger.

Hundreds of black wings flared and black beaks parted, calling for blood.

The trees rumbled and rattled in their holes, and an unkindness of ravens . . .

a congress of ravens . . .

a melee of ravens . . .

a cacophony of wings and claws and feathered shrieks all took to the air, a black attack on the sky, the vanguard of the storm.

Squid groveled on his belly as the tree behind him began to change. And the tree in front of him. And every tree he could see.

Starting at the dot of blood on the bark above Squid's head, the wood began to part and widen into a doorway large enough for a child to enter—or a hunching adult. Four doors opened in the tree—one at each point of the compass—but they didn't connect. Four to a tree, but each releasing its own air, its own smells. They were all doors into darkness. The heartwood was gone. Or hidden.

The tremors stopped. The trees had been remade. And then the ravens descended, screaming.

Black birds swooped for every door, diving without hesitation into darkness—two into the door above Squid.

And as they disappeared, the army of men advanced.

It seemed to take no time at all before a single raven reemerged from a tree, trumpeting discovery, fluttering above a doorway, calling all hunters to come and see what had been found.

Men with blades and moving mushrooms raced forward. The men who smelled of fire followed after.

But Squid was distracted. From the door behind him, he smelled something unknown and mysterious and very alive. Alive and angry and . . . interesting.

Turning his back on the attack behind him, he nosed forward into the cool air in the tree, snorting and sniffing.

LAWRENCE WAS TRYING NOT to cry. After all, he was with his parents, even if they were all in a strange stone hallway while angry men with old-fashioned guns and heavy shields waited for two other men to cut the iron door down with flames so they could attack his sister and his friends.

Behind the gunners, there were three shapes—he assumed they were men—wearing floor-length black chain-mail sheets without eyeholes or mouth holes. They each held a brassy net like a weapon.

Robert Boone turned away from the door and looked at the Smiths.

"You should leave," he said. "Get your son out of here."

"We will not," Albert growled. "My daughter is in there. If you try to hurt her, blood will be spilled, boy. Mine or yours, I don't care which, as long as it isn't hers."

"Robert," Thor growled. "You're overreacting."

Robert met the big man's gaze, and Lawrence moved a little closer to his father.

"Way-magic has been conducted on these grounds already," Robert said. "If you have enabled more of the old ways to be opened, it is not possible for one in my position to overreact. Judgment will be swift and final. And I will stand before the Sages of this Order with a clear conscience."

Iron popped and squealed as flames finally parted the hinges. The heavy door dropped its weight onto the stone floor with a boom that rolled away down the long hall.

Robert Boone drew both of his guns and cocked the hammers with his thumbs.

"Heave!" he yelled. "Set the door aside!"

Many hands obeyed.

Trudie pulled Lawrence tight and grabbed her husband's hand as the room opened.

The men with shields braced for assault, but none came.

The room held nothing but a single raven, fluttering around the beams, and as they watched, the bird dove into an open sarcophagus cupboard, and its cries ceased.

Robert Boone shoved his way into the room, turning in a slow circle beside the table, scanning the door and the cupboard-lined walls.

"Albert," Trudie whispered from behind Lawrence. "Tell me she's okay."

Albert said nothing.

Thor crossed his arms and exhaled loudly, clearly relieved.

Robert Boone swept the lightning frames off the table onto the floor.

"Smiths!" he bellowed. "You will answer for everything your daughter has done."

And mushroom hunters and blade slaves poured out of the sarcophagus into the room.

Hyacinth was sitting on an enormous fallen tree, gray and dry and smooth. It had a crack in its belly that she and the brothers had managed to exit with a fair amount of wriggling, and she was instantly grateful that she had chosen the door she had.

She had chosen a large Japanese door, with wide dark planks clearly milled from a single tree and small inset windowpanes made of mother of pearl, mostly because it had a large amount of wood for her to work with. But it had also been the most beautiful door in the room. And it had led her to a beautiful place.

The lake island was tall, dotted with smooth boulders and rugged trees. It smelled like moss and rain and . . . barn. Animals. But she heard no bird and saw no beast. The lake water licked at beaches of round stone, and a crisp breeze came and went, shifting the scent.

Mordecai and Caleb had gone exploring, giving Hyacinth the chance to sit in a moment of peace and attempt to process what her future might be. She wasn't sure. And that was all that she was sure of.

When an enormous fern moved at the end of her log, she assumed the brothers had returned with their report and they would be forced to discuss plans. Instead, an animal appeared. It froze, staring at her with a perceptiveness that she had rarely encountered in humans.

The animal was the color of an old slate blackboard, with chalk traces that would never be removed. It was low-slung on four legs and built like a short-legged, wide-bodied dog. It had scaly, baggy skin, a blunted horn on its nose, tiny sharp eyes, and dark feathered wings that would have been large on an eagle.

"What are you?" Hyacinth asked out loud. "A flying rhino? Are you full grown?"

Despite the horn, she had no fear of the animal. Although it clearly also had no fear of her.

She wanted to slide off the log and hug the creature, scratching and rubbing its dry skin until she found the spots that would make it groan and roll onto its back. But the seriousness of the animal stopped her. It was obviously passing judgment on her, and it was doing so with an extreme solemnity, a dignity that defied the creature's comic construction.

"Well," Hyacinth said. "Do I pass?" She smiled, still resisting the temptation to move from her perch.

The animal flared wide rhinocerine nostrils and puffed at the air.

Hyacinth heard more puffing behind her.

Spinning around, she found herself face to face with two more, seated on the log only three feet from her. These two were paler—the chalk on the board rather than the board—and their horns had seen less battle. Both of them had their noses in the air and their beady eyes on Hyacinth. The breeze rustled cloud-colored feathers on their upstretched wings.

Hyacinth wanted to laugh out loud, but she knew that laughter would be highly offensive. At least right now.

A dozen more snouts puffed around her.

Slowly, she scanned her surroundings. There seemed to be one or two of the creatures on every rock—various shades of gray, various sizes, but all watching her. Two, no, three so small they had to be from a fresh litter. Another virtually hornless with tattered wings, the size of a solid pig.

And only the first of them had made any noise upon arrival. Clearly, it had been intentional. They had watched her until they were ready to be noticed. Until they had gathered a great enough force.

Hyacinth felt fear try to climb up her throat, but she immediately forced it away and focused on friendship.

I'm a friend. I'm loyal. I'm kind and gentle and I will harm no one.

That wasn't true. And she couldn't lie to these things. She could see that in their eyes.

I harm only enemies. Only those I must.

And then two croaking ravens exploded out of the crack in the log between her feet.

Hyacinth screamed, rocked backward, and fell.

Dead wood and ferns and moss all crumpled beneath her. The impact was hard, but not hard enough to steal her breath. All around her, animals were bellowing and the air was filled with the beating of many wings.

Hyacinth rolled onto her knees and climbed quickly to her feet, looking over the fallen log at a great deal of chaos in the air.

At least fifteen of the heavy winged animals were pursuing the ravens out over the lake. They weren't fast, but they were efficient, and they were clearly of one mind. Fanning out in a wide crescent, they corralled the black-feathered birds back toward the island.

But one of the hunters wasn't in pursuit. Instead, he was climbing as high as he could—heavy slate body drooping between his large goose wings.

The ravens dropped low, croaking in panic, flapping frantically back toward the island and Hyacinth and the crack in the fallen log.

The high-flying hunter stopped climbing. He tucked his wings in tight to his wide body, and dove.

Part dart, part meteor, the animal fell with deadly purpose. The other hunters fell silent, and the rattling cries of the ravens were suddenly alone.

The two black birds were still over the lake when the heavy animal smashed through the lead raven in a cloud of feathers and then hit the water like a bomb.

The splash rose up in a plume, rolling the second raven onto its side and sending it veering into thick brush on the island's bank. As the rest of the hunters closed in, the bird fought free of the brush and managed to get back off the ground, desperately flapping straight up the island at the fallen tree in front of Hyacinth.

"No!" Hyacinth yelled. Belly hopping up onto the log, she tried to throw her arms in front of the crack, but her reach was too short.

The wet raven vanished into the tree. Half a heartbeat later, wide wings and a young horn and chalky skin vanished after it, billowing air up around Hyacinth's face.

The island was suddenly calm. Scrambling back up onto her perch, Hyacinth looked around, breathing hard.

The animals were all back on the ground, motionless, with noses in the breeze and wings uplifted. And then the big meteoric hunter rose out of the water, wading up the bank with slow solemnity. The dead and dripping raven dangled from his mouth, and as he laid its body on a rock and spat out feathers, three piglet-size copies of himself scrambled out of the bushes and raced forward. While the dripping conqueror attempted to spit out the feathers stuck on his pale pink tongue, the young ones tore into the carcass around his feet.

Carnivores, Hyacinth thought. *That isn't reassuring. Not at all.*

SQUID HAD HIS HEAD and shoulders all the way inside the tree when the raven darted out above him with the wide-winged light gray creature snapping right behind it.

166

When the gray creature grabbed the raven in its jaws and tumbled to the ground, Squid hopped around on all three legs, unsure of how to respond. An enemy of an enemy wasn't always a friend. But whatever the creature was, it didn't seem at all bothered by the wounded dog, or by the hundreds of other trees with gaping doors, or by the armed men and wizards swarming around one tree in particular. With the raven still flopping in its mouth, the animal tucked its wings in tight and walked calmly back toward Squid, past Squid, and then into the tree.

While men yelled and ravens swirled, Squid's caution was devoured by his canine curiosity.

Sniffing long and hard, with eyes strained wide and ears thrown forward, the wounded dog limped into the open door.

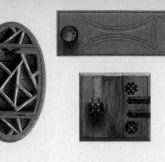

ELEVEN

TRUDIE HAD MANAGED TO shove Lawrence into an
alcove that held black suits of armor under dusty sheets.
She pushed him to the ground and crouched in front of
him, but the battle raging in the hallway was only a dozen
feet away. It rattled the bones of the building and shattered
windows with the noise.

Ravens combed the ceiling above both sides, croaking out their battle cry. One after another, they swooped
into the alcove, fluttered around as they eyed Lawrence,
dodging Trudie's blows before veering back out above the
melee.

Lawrence had never seen or heard anything like it. He
wasn't sure he ever would again. He had his hands pressed
over his ears, but his fear and his grief about Hyacinth had
vanished, replaced entirely with wonder and adrenaline.

Defenders with shields had interlocked them to form a
wall, and they'd dropped their bodies low to brace against
the onslaught. Whenever one began to crumple, he called
out and another man crawled forward to help him.

Behind the bodies and the shields, Albert Smith and Robert Boone and a dozen others wielded guns. Firing and firing and firing until the gunshots and the echoes all became one.

Thor was covered in blood and singing in another language, and even his huge voice could barely penetrate the chaos.

The Viking stood in the center of the hallway, holding two black maces, and whenever the double-mouthed monsters or men with long blades managed to leap the shield wall, it was Thor who ended them with a blow. The real men crumpled quickly, but the mushroom men didn't stop chewing and biting and clawing until they were in pieces and trampled to pulp.

From both sides of the hallway, more fighters came. Men and women with suntans and boots and shotguns behind the shield wall; mushroom monsters and blade slaves from the other.

"Forward!" Robert Boone shouted, but no one heard him.

"Forward!" Thor bellowed, and all at once, the shields were lifted and the shield-bearers drove the wall forward into the attackers with as much force as they could muster. A mushroom man as tall as Robert but with a waist as thin as Lawrence's leapt the wall with both mouths gaping and arms outstretched.

A single swing tore him in two, and one half slid

sloppily into the alcove. Trudie pulled Lawrence farther away, pressing him against the wall.

"Forward!" Thor bellowed again, and the shield wall obeyed. Fewer foes leapt over the top. Fewer guns fired.

"Forward!" Robert Boone shouted, and this time every fighter heard him. "Push! To the doorway! Seal them inside."

The shield wall advanced out of Lawrence's sight. As did his father and Boone and the Viking. The men and women in front of him now were unbloodied and tense in reserve.

From outside and all around, Lawrence could hear bells pealing in alarm.

"Did we win?" he asked his mother. "Is it over?"

A storm of ice crystals swept through the hallway, tearing skin and clothes and gathering screams of pain.

"Not yet," Trudie said. "We have to run. Now. While we can." She dragged Lawrence forward, but he grabbed his mother's wrists and pulled her back. Something was coming. Something bad.

The ice was followed by a rolling cloud of fire at head height. Ravens dropped to the ground smoking. The screaming heightened. Some of the reserves turned and ran. The rest pressed into the alcove, crushing Lawrence and Trudie against the back wall.

Trudie hugged her son tight.

"Dear God, be with them," she whispered. And Lawrence heard her with his ear pressed to her ribs. She looked down at him. "Thank you." Her eyes were wide and fearful. "How did you know?"

Lawrence didn't have time to answer. He hadn't known. He had felt.

And then both of his eardrums burst. Bodies spun down the hallway, swept by a wall of wind, and the first beams fell from the ceiling.

HYACINTH WATCHED AS THE second raven was chewed slowly by two midsize hornless animals. The rest of the animals watched as well, all with hunger in their eyes.

And then Squid, bloody and gimpy, tumbled out of the fallen tree and sprawled in a fern. In an instant, every head turned. A few wings flared.

"No!" Hyacinth slid down and scooped the sticky dog up in her arms. "Not for food."

The animals stared at her and at the dog, and their eyes told her very little. The creatures seemed bored by her display. The big one, still damp from his dive into the lake, actually yawned.

"Well, haven't you just made a flour-cake fool of yourself?"

Hyacinth looked back up at the log. Where she had just been sitting, a small, thick-bodied man was now standing.

He had round cheeks and a round nose and thick hair bushing straight up from his skull like a hair volcano, frozen in mid-eruption.

"Do you have any knowledge of the beasts at all, or are you daft clear through your girlie skull?"

"Excuse me?" Hyacinth shook her head. "I don't understand."

"Truth from the thieftess." He laughed. "How can you not know raggants but find your way here? This island has no pilgrims but those seeking the beasties. Have you even brought a sack? Where's your coracle?"

"I'm not here to steal an animal," Hyacinth said. "I'm sorry. I don't know what a coracle is, and I didn't bring a sack." She faced the little man, still holding Squid. "They're called raggants? Is that what you said?"

The man cocked his head and raised an eyebrow thicker than any caterpillar she had ever seen. Then he gathered the hair on top of his head and pulled it straight out on both sides. When he let go of it, the hair stayed, as stiff as wire.

"Indeed. Raggant is what I said because raggant is what they be. Is the isle called for the beasts or the beasts for the isle?" He shrugged. "No faerie could say and not be lying. But you stand on the soil of Raggant Isle, so named for as long as any creature knows, and if you are not here to steal a beast, then I would love to hear whatever tale you may care to tell to explain you standing here in plain sight of all eyes present. True or false, tell it how you like. I've been here nine and a half moons and have heard no voice but my own and the songs of the beasties when they're calling up the fish."

When he finished, he shoved his thick fingers into his pockets and stared at Hyacinth.

She set Squid down on the ferns and glanced around to be sure that he was in no danger. Then she focused her attention back on the man above her.

"My name is Hyacinth," she said. "What's yours?"

"Oh, ho," the little man said. "You're quick to pry. I'll answer to Kibs if your voice needs a handle, but I'll tell you no more except to say that I belong to Mound Nine of Glaston, and the Central Committee of Faeren currently has no desire for my presence. Thus, I have been appointed ragherd of this rumpus, and guardian of this isle." He snorted. "Not that they need herding, nor the isle guarding. But the beasties tolerate me."

"Kibs," Hyacinth said. "Very nice to meet you. I'm here partly by accident and partly because I was trying to escape."

"Escape what?" Kibs asked. "From whither and why?"

Hyacinth laughed.

"And how?" Kibs added. His face was quite serious.

"First, from my home," Hyacinth said, erasing her laughter. She almost mentioned Mordecai and Caleb and then thought better of it. One thing at a time. "Through

173

a doorway in a tree. And then through an actual door I found hanging on a wall. I was running from an awful woman who would have killed me."

Kibs put his hands behind his back and leaned forward, staring into Hyacinth's eyes.

"A doorway in a tree?" He pursed his lips. "A doorway of your own spellcraft? And another door that led you here? If you are a witch, then we are foes, not friends, and your destruction will be swift." He pulled his hands from his pockets and cracked his lumpy knuckles.

"No spells," Hyacinth said quickly. "Not a witch. Not at all. I was running from a witch."

"Were those her ravens?" Kibs asked.

"Maybe," Hyacinth said. "Probably. I honestly don't know. Will you answer a question? What did you do to get sent here? You must have done something if your people didn't want you around."

Kibs stared at her, silent. Then he puffed his cheeks out and vanished.

"Whoa," Hyacinth said, taking a step back, and then a thunderous blow to her ribs sent her tumbling through the brush.

"Who are you to question me?" Kibs screamed. "A girl, a lassie, a brat, a human!"

Gasping, Hyacinth sat up, but the little man was still hidden.

"If you never leave this island, who will miss you?"

Kibs asked. "Will your mother grieve? I want your mother to grieve!"

"Faerie!" Mordecai crashed through the brush and stood in front of the log. Caleb followed him but hurried to help Hyacinth up.

All around, the raggants quietly disappeared. She couldn't see Kibs anywhere, but Mordecai was focused on something.

"Ooh, hoo!" Kibs laughed. "A game, a game. Here's some real sport! Catch me if you can, boyo!"

Mordecai's hand flamed, sprouting a vine behind it like a whip, and Kibs suddenly appeared, mouth open, fat cheeks flushed, eyes wide.

"Wait," Kibs said, raising both hands. "Please let me explain."

"Come here, faerie," Mordecai said. "You owe me loyalty."

"I didn't know she was with a green. I couldn't know. She didn't say."

"Does it matter?" Mordecai asked. "I said come, faerie. Speak to me eye to eye."

Hyacinth rubbed the spot on her ribs. Nothing broken, but she would have a mighty bruise.

Kibs was shuffling toward Mordecai, and his eyes were flashing with fury and worry, first one, then the other. Hyacinth could tell that he was deciding whether to fight.

But before the faerie could make up his mind,

Mordecai snapped the vine fire whip that had been dripping from his arm, and a cage of green and purple fire appeared in the air around a very surprised Kibs.

Mordecai looked back at Caleb and grinned.

"Maybe," Caleb said. "But he is hardly as powerful as the witch-queen. Still, let him test it."

"Witch-queen?" Kibs asked. "The witch-queen? Nimroth's daughter?"

"The same," Mordecai said. "Now, foolish faerie, let us see your full strength. Every drop of wrath you can muster. Break free of this cage and I'll forget that you disrespected a green man."

Kibs didn't have to be told twice. In a blur of smoke and wind and fire, he attacked the fiery vines above and around him.

The greens grew brighter, the purples deeper, but the faerie achieved nothing. Finally, panting and exhausted, Kibs collapsed in the center of his cage.

"If you were Nimiane of Endor," Mordecai said, "what would you do?"

"I would drink the life from the very ground," Kibs said. "I would summon the demons in my veins, and I would consume this cage and these trees and every living creature on this island."

"Try," Mordecai said.

Kibs rolled onto his side and glared at him.

"You've already been banished," Mordecai said. "Drink life from the ground and hurl it at me. I am Mordecai Westmore, the seventh son of Amram Iothric, and I tell you truly, there I will hold you guilty for it. You will be helping me."

"That is the path of darkness," Kibs said. "I wandered old ways through many worlds, breaking oaths and treaties and terrifying humans, but I have never set my feet on the paths of darkness."

"Sounds pretty dark to me," Hyacinth said.

Kibs wasn't listening. He jumped up and extended his hands toward the ground within his cage. The ferns and moss beneath his feet shriveled into ash, and he hurled every drop of the life he'd gathered at the fiery vines around him.

They brightened but didn't bend.

The faerie fell onto the ashen ground and began to cry.

"It works," Mordecai said, looking at his brother.

"It holds a breeze," Caleb said. "But it must hold a storm."

Mordecai stepped forward and gripped the nearest fiery vine. The cage collapsed at his touch.

"How?" Kibs asked, sitting up. "Your soul itself was in that fire."

"Yes," Mordecai said, and his voice was weary. "My life. My strength turned inside out—the vine roots inward, drinking what is enclosed, strengthening the whole. The attack is swallowed, the cage strengthened. Now apologize to the girl."

"The girl?" Hyacinth asked. "Excuse me?"

Mordecai smiled.

Kibs stumbled all the way over to her. The top of his head was barely higher than her waist.

"Hyacinth," he said, bowing. "Flower of mankind. Forgive my grievous and violent trespass."

Hyacinth wasn't sure if she was being mocked.

"I'll think about it," she said, and she looked at Caleb. "Now what are we doing?"

"We are going to trap the witch," Caleb said.

"We're going to try," Mordecai added.

"You're going to die," Kibs said. "I swear it by all of my finest meals."

Caleb and Mordecai both grimaced.

"You would need a place of complete death," Kibs said. "Dry of life. As barren as the moon. If you trap the queen with her Blackstar blood in the way you just trapped me, she will drink life from all around, not just from within the cage. If there is life anywhere within her reach, she will draw on it. If there is enough life, she will draw on it until she can break your viny soul bonds. Nimroth's spawn cannot and will not die."

"We know," Caleb said. "But she can be bound and buried and forgotten."

"Forgotten?" Kibs snorted at the foolishness of the word. "Nimiane will never be forgotten."

"You know," Mordecai said, looking at Caleb, "there's only one place we can do this."

Caleb nodded. "Sadly."

"Where?" Hyacinth asked. "The moon?"

"Might as well be," Caleb said. "There is no land so dead as the land in old Endor. Nimroth's first city."

Kibs laughed. "Walk in that land and you have died already."

Mordecai faced the faerie, crossing his arms.

"Faerie," he said. "Where does your loyalty lie?"

Irritated, Kibs pushed his wiry hair into a spike off the back of his head.

"I am loyal to my family." Kibs was practically a monotone, like a schoolboy droning off a memorized and disliked answer. "To the faeren of my mound. To their allies, and to the Central Committee of my race, and abide by all the treaties and conventions and manuals by them issued and adopted."

"Good answer," Mordecai said. "What of the green bloods?"

Kibs sniffed. "My mound swore loyalty to the green man, Amram Iothric," he muttered.

"And?" Caleb asked.

"And his blood," Kibs answered.

"Am I his blood?" Mordecai asked.

Kibs squinted at him, then sniffed again. "You are."

"Then I require your service," Mordecai said. "Your banishment is waived and your crimes forgiven. You will guide us on the old roads of your people, wherever we may need to go."

"To Endor?" Kibs sighed. "I would rather remain with the rumpus of raggants on this island for all eternity."

Mordecai laughed.

"Your rathering doesn't matter," Caleb said. "Load a pack. We can't afford to wait long."

The faerie lived in a small stone hut on the other side of the island. The roof was shaggy sod, the floor was dirt, and so was the back wall. As it turned out, he didn't have much to pack. He grabbed a small block of old cheese, a long knife, and a knobby stick.

"All right," Kibs said. "Let's see if we can get through."

Approaching the back wall, he thumped the dirt with the stick and then traced the outline of a door. After a moment he thumped the dirt again.

"There might not be anyone there," Kibs said. "No one comes through the banishment mounds unless they're dropping off food."

Mordecai stepped forward and raised his fiery palm.

"I wouldn't do that," Kibs said. "They'll take it personally."

"Fine by me," Mordecai said, and he banged on the dirt, shaking it like a drum.

"Kibs!" a muffled voice shouted. "Cease!"

Mordecai didn't cease.

And then the dirt vanished, opening into a many-sided room with a stone floor and a dirt roof, held up with interwoven roots.

Three faeren stood in the doorway, two slight and one stout and ruddy, all holding cudgels.

"Thank you," Mordecai said, and he stepped forward, beckoning Hyacinth and Caleb to follow him.

"Excuse me!" the stout faerie bellowed. "No humans in the mounds."

"I told them not to," Kibs said. "I did. I swear it."

"I am a green blood," Mordecai said. "Pauper son of the fallen Amram Iothric. You owe me your allegiance."

All three of the faeren puffed out their cheeks and vanished, at least to Hyacinth's eyes, and she immediately braced for an attack.

"I can still see you," Mordecai said. "As you well know. Resist me, and I will strike you down. And if you survive, I will charge you before the Central Committee."

The faeren reappeared, one at a time.

"What do you want?" the stout one asked.

"Passage," Mordecai said. "For myself, my brother, my friend, and my guide."

Hyacinth wasn't sure if she should interrupt. Did she need to travel with Mordecai into the witch's dead land?

"Guide?" the stout one said. "I see no guide."

"Kibs," Mordecai answered. "Against his will, he has been pressed into my service."

"I don't know." The faerie shook his head.

"You don't need to know," Caleb answered, and together, he and Mordecai pushed forward.

"Hold on," Hyacinth said. "I could wait here, couldn't I? You don't need me."

"We do need you," Mordecai said. "And you shouldn't stay with them without me. They owe you no loyalty, and they never pay what they don't owe."

The faeren parted, and Hyacinth hurried forward, crossing through the dirt door into the cool room on Mordecai's heels.

Kibs hesitated at the threshold, clearly unsure of what was about to happen to him.

"Where are you traveling?" the stout faerie asked.

"Where I like," Mordecai said. "And unquestioned, as is my right." He turned slowly, looking at the many dirt-filled doorways around the room. "Kibs?"

The faerie frantically mussed his hair, held his breath, and then stepped inside. Relieved, he exhaled, sputtering his lips.

"When you're ready," Mordecai said, "choose our first door."

TWELVE

LAWRENCE WAS RESTING ON his side in a small white hospital bed, watching the sun set over a huge lake. The window beside his bed was tall and cut into a thick stone wall. Thin white curtains had been pulled wide, and the window had been opened a little to let in the breeze.

He didn't know where he was, but it was beautiful. And it was hard to fully sleep. Every time his mind slipped away, he thought he heard a scream or a blast or he saw the beams falling. Sometimes the vision of Thor smashing a monster was waiting for him right behind his eyelids, and he would jerk in the bed and his eyes would fly open and the stitched-up gash on his head would ache and his mother would lean forward in her chair and touch him, whispering her love or singing softly, promising him that she was there and that everything would be all right.

His mother was covered with dust and black pasty patches where dust had mixed with blood. The rest of the beds in the high-ceilinged room were full, and doctors and nurses moved from one to the next.

"Gertrude Smith?" a nurse asked. "They are ready for you."

Lawrence twisted in his bed to see the nurse. The medicine he'd been given made her a little blurry, but she looked nice. And clean.

Trudie stood up, and Lawrence sat up quickly.

"I want to come," Lawrence said. "Please. I'm fine. It was just stitches."

"No," Trudie said. "Not for this. Stay and try to sleep." His mother bent and kissed his head. "And then pray. Pray for your sister." She didn't need to say which one.

Lawrence watched his weary mother leave, walking slowly between rows of beds. When she had gone, he lay back down and checked on the sun.

It was nothing but an afterglow now, and the light on the lake was vanishing.

As his eyes drooped, this time he was no longer in the battle in the hallway. He was with his sister.

TRUDIE WAS ESCORTED INTO a lush chamber by a man in formal dress, who also happened to be wearing a gun. The floor was gleaming wood. The walls were lined with portraits, and crystal chandeliers hung from polished black beams. Albert and Thor were both standing in the center of the room, facing a long, curving marble table. Behind the table, men and women—all with some degree of white hair and sun-aged skin—sat like statues.

Albert had his right arm in a sling, and Thor had his head wrapped with bandages and half of his beard burned off. Both had extensive burns on their clothes.

A younger man stood at the end of the table with his arms behind his back. He watched as Trudie hurried forward to her husband and slipped her arm under his.

"How's L?" he whispered.

"Fine," Trudie answered. "Worried."

Albert nodded.

The young man at the end of the table cleared his throat. "The Sages of the Order of Brendan have reached a decision in the case of Hyacinth Smith."

Trudie licked her dusty lips and waited.

"The girl, daughter of Albert and Gertrude Smith, opened ways and used them for travel, did she not?"

Albert nodded. "She did, but she had no knowledge that what she was doing was—"

The man interrupted him. "Forces unknown entered this estate in violence due to her actions, did they not?"

Albert nodded grimly.

Trudie looked down the length of the table, moving from gray-haired man to gray-haired woman, hoping to see some pity. Some flicker of understanding.

Every eye was hard. Every jaw was set.

"This intrusion was boldly repelled with great injury, and at the cost of seven lives thus far. Many more, including the life of this Order's Avengel, Robert Boone, remain in peril from their grievous wounds. The Room of Ways has been sealed and, until a greater force can be assembled, lost. Also, the former home of Isaac Smith, and current home of Albert and Trudie Smith, where the first ways were opened, shall henceforth be forbidden ground until sufficient strength can be mustered to search and cleanse the premises."

"May I speak?" Thor asked. The young man nodded. "The Smiths have been loyal and faithful. They themselves were engaged in the battle and fought bravely. Their young son is wounded; their daughter is missing and likely dead. The fault does not lie with them, or with their daughter. She was attacked due to the folly of a woman named Granlea Quarles, and she fled. She had no knowledge that the opening of ways was forbidden. In all likelihood, she did not know that the opening of ways was even possible. She fought for survival and fled for the same motive."

The young man cleared his throat, but an old man at the center of the table raised his hand. He had hollow brown cheeks and thin cobwebby hair. His eyes were small but bright.

"The actions of Ms. Quarles will be addressed. The rest of what you say has been considered. But if the girl did not know our laws, whose fault is that? If her gifts had never been assessed, whose fault is that?"

"Mine, sir," Albert said. "Entirely mine."

The old man nodded slowly. "Let me ask you this, Mr.

Smith. And you too, Mrs. Smith. Would not the Order have been better off if your daughter had not opened a way? Even if she and her brother had been killed, would not the loss of those two lives have been preferable—to the Order, if not to you—to the seven thus far fallen?"

Albert didn't answer. Trudie slipped her hand down into his and squeezed, biting her lip hard. She would not cry. She would not scream or collapse or flee the room. She would stand with her husband while they heard the worst.

The old man leaned back in his chair. The young man cleared his throat and resumed.

"If the girl, Hyacinth Smith, should be found alive, her life shall be forfeit. If any member of this Order should discover her location and not disclose it immediately to the Avengel, their life shall be forfeit. If any former member of this Order should discover her location and not disclose it immediately to the Avengel, their life shall be forfeit. Is this judgment clear?"

Albert said nothing. Trudie said nothing, but she felt like her heart had stopped beating. Her skin had turned to ice.

"Thank you," the young man said. "Dismissed. The wounded deserve your prayers."

"The judgment is clear," Thor said aloud as the men and women rose slowly from behind the table. "But not just." Turning, he leaned his head down between the two Smiths.

"I will take Lawrence to camp. He will be with his siblings and my Rupert. You"—he looked from one to the other—"go find your daughter."

HYACINTH HAD GRABBED ON to the back of Mordecai's shirt as they moved through darkness. Caleb gripped the back of hers, and Kibs led the way. Squid limped along behind them.

"The committee will have me skinned for this," the faerie muttered.

"No," Mordecai said. "They won't. I won't let them."

"Yes," Kibs said. "They will. Because you'll be dead and I'll be standing there with my fat hands in my empty pockets and an impossible tale to tell."

Mordecai was silent.

"Why did I do it?" Kibs asked. "Lovely question. I did it because the boy told me I wasn't banished anymore and he required my services. What services, you ask? Why, guidance down the forbidden roads into the forbidden land to fight the queen of all that is unholy, of course. I'm sure you'd have done the same in my slippers, Chairman Radulf, no doubt about it."

"Will you be silent?" Caleb asked. "Where are we now?"

"Dodging quickly through what was once the central mound," Kibs replied. "And why not? It's only been cursed for a century or two, since Nimiane threw down her father and set out to drink us dry. We're getting closer. Only a hop or two more and all your dreams will come true. Kibs will set your feet in the deadest of all the deadest lands, huzzah, hurrah, and oodahlay."

"We'll need a place with an exit," Mordecai said.

The parade suddenly stopped in the darkness and Hyacinth banged into Mordecai's back, her face colliding with the hard fungal teeth beneath his shirt. He flinched in pain but said nothing.

"Sorry," she whispered.

"What?" Kibs asked. "I don't understand. An exit?"

Mordecai threw a thin gold vine up into the air, lighting the room. The vine attached to the ceiling, dozens of feet up, and Hyacinth looked around at what had been hidden in darkness.

"Wow," Caleb said quietly behind her. "I hadn't expected it to be so . . . big."

The room was circular, domed, and terraced in rings, descending to a hole in the floor at the center. The interwoven old roots in the roof had died and collapsed in places.

"Don't use light," Kibs said. "Please."

"Why?" Mordecai asked. "What have we to fear?"

"All the things that might choose to travel through a place like this," Kibs answered. "None of them pleasant."

"Things like us," Caleb said.

"Right," said Kibs. "Exactly what I was thinking. Terrifying things like children seeking destruction."

"An exit," Mordecai said. "I know the faeren had secret ways in and out of her dead lands. My father said you spy on your enemies almost as much as you spy on your friends."

Kibs snorted and rubbed his nose, looking around the open space nervously.

"Do you see this, green man? This death? This is what comes from having doors into the dead lands. In the beginning, we had many and we stole much—cupboards and cabinets, wardrobes and bookshelves. Now the great doors are all that remain. The others were severed. The witch-queen leached our lives even through doors she could not see."

Wings flapped on the other side of the domed room, just beyond a mound of collapsed ceiling.

Every head turned. Squid began to growl.

On the outskirts of the light, Hyacinth saw black-feathered wings gliding. And then a raven croaked.

Caleb set an arrow on his bowstring.

"If that raven escapes," Kibs said, "she'll know we're coming, yes?"

"Maybe," Mordecai said. "Or it's just a bird."

The raven's croaking grew louder and multiplied.

"So much for that theory," Hyacinth said. "There's

more than one. We should have brought some of those raggants. They ate two ravens on the island."

She could see three. Four.

"Six," Caleb said. "And more coming."

Squid began to bark.

"All right, Kibs," Mordecai said. "Now we hurry."

NIMIANE MANAGED TO CRAWL back to the rocking chair, past the body of Granlea Quarles. When two of her witch-dogs entered the room to report, she saw the horror in their eyes as they looked at her. Both men drew away, but when she pointed her finger bone up at the chair, they stepped forward and lifted her beneath her arms.

Fools.

As they touched her, she desperately drank of their lives. The men wavered, weakened, and stumbled away when they set her down. She couldn't see them, but she knew them by their smell and taste. One was bald, with a thick black beard. The other had his head shorn and was too young for hair of any kind on his face.

She couldn't waste strength on her appearance, but she could speak. Barely.

"Report," she said, and her voice was like a wind moving over an empty glass.

She heard the men straighten.

"The birds found the boy of this family," the bald man said. "And traces of the girl. We pursued with full force but were met by an ambush, well armed, well positioned. We were pushed back."

The witch could only gasp her anger, but from the smell the men both gave off, she knew her fury was made clear.

"A century of mushroom hunters have been lost," the young man said. "And three dozen blades. We can spare them, but the way has been closed."

"Not closed," the bald man said quickly. "The other side has been sealed in a secure room. We have withdrawn fully, and I have sent the birds searching the other ways."

Bast. Nimiane needed her cat. Where were her eyes? She sent her mind roaming for the feline's mind. She wanted to see these men when she killed them. Then, with their strength in her own legs, she herself would venture into the ways.

Outside, ravens began croaking wildly. The voices of men called out in excitement.

"Majesty," the bald man said. And she listened to both witch-dogs run from the house.

Bast. Nimiane reached for her. *Bast.*

And suddenly Nimiane's mind was bright, full of scent and taste and light, and very far away. Her face was low, and her tongue was licking blood up from a stone floor.

"Come." Nimiane spoke the word loudly in her mind, but the sound barely crossed her lips.

The cat rose from her drink. She was coming.

THE SOUND OF RAVENS was becoming a storm in the chambers behind them, but it was getting harder for Hyacinth to hear over her breathing.

Still holding on to Mordecai's shirt, Hyacinth was running. Behind her, Caleb was trying not to step on her feet.

Wings beat the air as a shape passed above her, and Hyacinth had already learned what came after ravens.

"Not far," Kibs said, and they veered left.

Hyacinth couldn't see the doorway, but she knew when they passed through. The temperature rose. The air dried.

"Hold on," Mordecai said, and they staggered to a stop. "That doorway . . ." He was panting. Only Kibs seemed unaffected by the effort.

"Was a four-hundred-mile leap south," Kibs answered. "Two more miles on foot, and then another seven or eight hundred if we can't open the doorway."

"We'll open it." Mordecai's hand blazed. "I should close this one behind us. If they're coming . . ."

"Please do," Hyacinth said. "I don't want to be grabbed from behind in the dark."

"Outrun them, green blood. Outrun them!" Kibs was insistent. "Save your strength. There won't be much to draw on where we're heading."

"He's right," Caleb said. "We should run."

Lit only by the light rising from his hand, Mordecai stood tall, gathering his breath.

"All right," he said. "Hy?"

"I'm good," Hyacinth said. "I can keep going."

Her bare feet were throbbing, but at least the floors had been fairly smooth.

Echoing in the darkness behind them, they heard something much louder than wings.

Feet.

And voices.

"Maybe we should start right now," Hyacinth said.

Caleb laughed, and Mordecai cracked a small smile. Forming back up in their train, two boys and a girl ran into the darkness behind a faerie.

One minute later, Squid collapsed in the doorway, straddling the two temperatures. He could smell the way his pack people had gone. That was easy enough. But he knew there was no way he would be catching them.

Hyacinth had tried to carry him when they had first started, but he had wriggled and fought free, forcing her to put him down.

Hunted people didn't need to be slower because of a fat wounded dog.

Behind him, he could smell what was coming. There were the many birds. And the mushrooms. And the men. But out in front of them all, running silently, Squid caught the scent of wolf.

Birds could be ignored. Men could be fought. But Squid knew the wolf would catch his pack. It would attack from the darkness in silence and pull the girl down by the throat. She would not know it was coming. She would have no time to fight or scream.

Squid shifted his body around and backed through the doorway.

This was better. Being carried was not what Squid was for. Running many miles was not for him either. Neither was surviving.

He lowered his body to the floor and envisioned his movement—leaping up from the ground, his jaws would find wolf throat. He would close them, and he would never let go. Never.

The wolf would not reach his pack. That was all.

Squid rested his jaw on his paws and closed his eyes, smelling. Listening.

He knew it would be soon. And he was ready.

WELL BEHIND THEM IN the darkness, Hyacinth heard the sudden desperate snarling. Pulling Mordecai to a stop, she turned.

The snarling became a desperate howl as claws scraped and stone clattered.

"Squid," Hyacinth said, and sadness flooded her.

"That's not the dog," Caleb said. "That's a wolf. The dog is winning."

Mordecai pulled Hyacinth forward.

"Come on," he said. "He just gave us time. We have to use it!"

SQUID HAD JUMPED UP at the smell. His jaws had closed on the big animal's throat. And then the thrashing had begun.

Claws tore into Squid's back. Into his belly. The wolf snarled and shook and twisted and rolled and howled.

Squid closed his eyes and felt nothing but the strength in his own grip and the salty flood pouring over his jaws.

The wolf snapped at his back legs. At his spine. But Squid only squeezed tighter.

By the time the wolf staggered and fell, panting his last, Squid had forgotten that he was even there. He was back on the island with the winged horns. And Shark and Ray were there too, and they barked and beckoned to Squid to play.

THE DOOR INTO OLD Endor was big and black and dry, lined with deep rotten cracks, like burned wood, though no fire had touched it.

Touching it made Hyacinth feel ill, but Mordecai asked her to. He needed her help opening the doors. And so she swallowed down the bile that climbed up her throat, and she sent her mind into the dead wood.

There was no life to awaken. There was not even the ghost of life—no way for her to sense what kind of a tree it had been or find a single ring, a grain, a shred of time or memory.

"It's not just dead," Hyacinth said. "It's like it never lived."

"How do we open it?" Caleb asked.

"We don't," Kibs said. "No key to this lock. No hinge to this door. The way was sealed, but even this—the seal—is now dead. Kick it in and I will leave you here, my duty done."

Mordecai stepped back and then sent a fiery vine plunging through the rotten wood. Ripping it back, a three-foot slab of death fell into the darkness.

Moonlight poured in through the hole, and to Hyacinth's fast-blinking eyes, it was as bright as searing flame.

"I still need you, Kibs," Mordecai said. "But this I shouldn't command. From here, if you come, it is of your own free will. That is how my father always treated the faeren, and I hope to do the same."

"How your father always treated us when?" Kibs asked.

"Whenever he went knocking on death's own door," Mordecai said. "Stay and see how this adventure ends. Or don't. I won't judge you."

Kibs shuffled in place and sniffed. Then he jerked a thumb at Caleb.

"But he will," he said. "He'll judge me."

"That's right," said Caleb. "I'll write a song about the coward Kibs and sing it to queens."

Hyacinth laughed.

"And if I come?" Kibs asked. "What will you sing then?"

"Nothing," said Caleb. "I'll pretend you weren't even here."

"That's cruel," Hyacinth said, but she was smiling. She grabbed Kibs's jacket and pulled him around to face her. "I forgive you for hitting me," she said. "And if you come with us now and we succeed, I will make sure Caleb tells the truth about you."

"I don't care about that," Kibs said. "Will you make me a pie?"

"Pie," Hyacinth said, surprised. "I've never made pie, but my mother has. Often. I can learn."

"I want a pie," Kibs said. "For Christmas every year, for as long as we're both alive."

"Deal." Hyacinth nodded. "Any fruit you like."

"Well then," Kibs muttered. "Let's go hunting witches."

The faerie tugged his jacket free, shuffled to the doorway, and hopped through the hole into old Endor.

Mordecai and Caleb followed.

Hyacinth held back for a moment, facing the darkness.

"Goodbye, Squid," she said. "And thank you."

THIRTEEN

THE CITY SLEPT UNDER a coating of dust, cool and soft beneath Hyacinth's feet. The streets were empty. Towers had crumbled. Windows stared at the moon like doorways into emptiness.

They hadn't stopped hurrying, following Kibs up hills and side streets, working their way toward a block of pillared buildings that could have once been palaces. Now they looked like sand castles built too high above the waterline, ignored by the waves and left to dissolve slowly in the sun.

And the moon.

Glancing back, Hyacinth watched the dust drift and settle in their wake. In the distance, she could see the little square with the dry fountain and the stone arch and door that they had entered.

She was sure that the shapes of hunters would emerge from it soon. And when they did, the path she and the others were leaving in the dust would not be hard to follow.

There had been other shapes—hooded human shapes

wandering in madness, one standing frozen in a window, another swaying and rocking slowly in a circle.

"Where are we going?" Caleb whispered.

Kibs pointed at a big shape with its face all in moon shadow.

"A royal dungeon, indeed," the faerie said. "Where Nimroth himself mutters through his centuries."

"Mordecai," Caleb said. "Our trail."

Mordecai turned and looked back over the dead city. "Maybe they'll be too frightened to follow."

"The birds, maybe," Caleb said. "Even ravens have their limit. But the men will come. And the hunters."

"We don't have time to make new trails," Hyacinth said. "If anyone is still following, they'll be here soon."

"Not a new trail," Mordecai said. "But maybe a bigger one." He raised his hand and his green vine light joined the light of the moon. He swept his arm around, and Hyacinth felt the air begin to move above her. Around and around, bigger and bigger, Mordecai grew a whirlwind.

Hyacinth was tired and hungry and frightened, but she almost laughed as the air on her face grew cold and fast. It was like watching a boy spin cotton candy with the wind.

The dust around them blew away, revealing crumbling cobblestone streets, stones so weak that they cracked softly under the weight of her bare feet.

And then Mordecai bowled the spinning wind down

into the city, swallowing every building in a cloud of dust, erasing the tracks left by four pairs of feet.

"Lovely," Caleb said. "I feel much better. Kibs, take us where you will."

NIMIANE SLEPT IN THE rocking chair with Bast on her lap. While her hunters hunted and her ravens searched through worlds and Hyacinth plodded barefoot through dust in the city of death, the witch's head lolled forward as she rested, as her strength slowly returned.

"Majesty."

The cat opened her eyes and looked up at the young witch-dog who had touched her earlier. But Nimiane did not move.

"They fled through old faeren roads," the man said. "We're on their heels. The sons of the dead green blood and the girl."

"The grower," the witch whispered. "The girl who opened ways."

"The same," the man said. "It will not be long now."

"Into what land?" the queen hissed. "In what world?"

The question made the man nervous. The cat twitched her ears, watching him sniff and shift his weight from foot to foot.

"Into Endor, Queen," he finally said. "Old Endor. They have entered the city."

"What?" Nimiane raised her head. "Why? How?"

"I do not know why, Queen," the man said. "But they entered through the old arch of the faeren. A raven was sent."

"Where in the city?" she asked. "Where? To the upper tombs? Those fools. Do they go to strike at my father?"

No, she thought. *They would not attack him. They would free him. Did they think Nimroth would be an ally? He would absorb them like raindrops. And then he would turn his ravening thoughts to her.*

Nimiane tried to rise to her feet, but she failed. The man stepped forward and offered her a hand.

She took it. She clasped it. And she fed.

When her hand was empty and his dust swirled around her feet, she stood with strength, and her appearance changed.

No longer the hag, Nimiane of Endor turned, facing the doorway in the wall that she had first entered, the door that led to her gardens that led to her city that led to the wasteland outside the walls that led to the old city and the prison tomb where she had robbed and entrapped her father, Nimroth the undying Blackstar.

Nimiane, witch-queen of Endor, entered her garden and stood in the moonlight.

Through the doorway behind her, in the strange world of California, even the sea sighed with relief.

WANDERING THE NARROW HALLS of countless prison wings, climbing stairs and descending stairs, Hyacinth hung back behind the group with her heart pounding in her ears.

There were voices here, muttering behind heavy doors in long-forgotten tongues.

Mordecai and Caleb discussed every room that appeared to be empty. When they slowly opened a room that wasn't empty, the jack-in-the-box screams of laughter stopped all their hearts. Caleb slammed the door with a boom like thunder, and now Kibs checked the doors with his nose and his ears before any were opened.

The empty rooms had thick stone walls devoid of life. All had heavy doors of lifeless iron. There were rags and occasionally ashen bones, but nothing else. Mordecai felt a cage could be made that would hold the witch. There was only one problem.

"No exits," Mordecai said. "We need a cell with two doors. One for her to enter, and one for our escape. If we're going to live."

"Living isn't the only option," Caleb whispered. He and his brother stepped around a corner, leaving Kibs and Hyacinth alone.

"Fools," Kibs muttered, but Hyacinth wasn't listening to him. She'd sent her hearing around the corner with the brothers.

"Yes," Mordecai said. "It is. You and I can choose to die, but I will not try this with no chance at life for her."

"Then send her away," Caleb said. "Send her with the faerie. He could get her clear if anyone could."

There was a long pause.

"You want her here," Caleb said. "But that's for you. Not her. Send them away. If this goes wrong, you and I can die together. We started this. The risk is all ours."

"She can't live with faeren."

"Then send her home. If we draw the witch here, her home may be fine."

Kibs looked up and down the dim and dark hallway, with moonlight trickling in through occasional iron grates. "Madness," he said. "This place is madness. I never thought I'd miss the smell of raggants."

Hyacinth walked past him, and then past the corner where the brothers were having their whisper. Someone had to keep looking. Descending a short stair and then climbing back up another, she went straight on again.

She paused at the first doors she came to. The tiny iron grate windows were too high for her to see through, so she simply jerked the heavy bolts and tugged the door open. A woman thinner than a skeleton was dancing in the center on a pile of rags.

Hyacinth slammed the door again and threw the bolt.

"What are you doing?" Mordecai hissed. Both brothers

and the faerie were staring at her from the top of the stairs behind her.

Hyacinth smiled and jerked the next door open. Nothing and no one. She slammed it and moved on.

Three more doors, none occupied. Four. Five. All emptiness.

"Hyacinth, stop," Mordecai said.

"You're not sending me away," she said. "And Caleb, thank you, but Kibs and I aren't best friends yet. I'm not traveling alone with him." She looked at Mordecai. "You need me. At least if you'd like to survive your own plan. And the risk isn't all yours, Caleb. You attacked the witch and then ran to my house. If you haven't forgotten, that changed a few things for me and my family. Since you went on your little quest, I think the Smiths have risked and lost a lot more than you have."

"Hyacinth," Caleb said.

"Stop." Hyacinth assessed the next door. It had no iron grate at all. And there were two dead bolts instead of one.

"Just listen," Caleb said.

Hyacinth didn't. She jerked the locks open and then put her foot against the wall and pulled. The iron hinges woke slowly, but they obeyed. Hyacinth stared into darkness with no windows at all, and she saw absolutely nothing.

The smell told her that someone was inside. So did the breathing. And the sound of scratching.

"Light, please," she said, and Mordecai stepped in beside her, raising his glowing palm.

A man and a woman were inside the room. The woman was scratching at a large slab of something in the floor, and the man was hunched over, perfectly still.

"Shut it," Mordecai said.

Hyacinth stopped his hand. Behind the two shapes, she'd found what she wanted.

"Everybody out!" Hyacinth said. "It's your lucky day. Free at last."

The man's head turned slowly toward her. The woman kept scratching.

Hyacinth looked at Mordecai. "This is the one," she said. "Get them out."

While Mordecai stepped inside and herded the two undying prisoners to their feet, Hyacinth slipped around the edge of the room and focused on the back wall. There was a shelf. And on the shelf, there was a box. And shelf and box were both made of wood.

Fearful, worried that they might be as drained of life as the great doorway they used to enter the city, Hyacinth gently touched them both.

The shelf was cedar. The box was ebony. The shelf was almost as dry as the dust on the floor, but the box still held . . . itself. A grain. Time and the stories of a thousand different days—stories shared by wood in other faraway places, hopefully less horrible than this one—were still present enough for Hyacinth to feel them, even if she couldn't read them.

But the door was tiny, no more than a cupboard.

"Kibs," Hyacinth said, "I'm going to need some faerie help, I think."

The faerie hopped into the room as the two shapes shuffled away.

"Not permitted," Kibs said. "Assisting a human in the creation of ways is . . . . is . . . ."

"I'm sure," Hyacinth said. "But you're already an outlaw. And I won't be creating anything. This wood is already connected to wood like it all over the worlds. I just need one of those connections to work."

"Who taught you this?" the faerie asked.

"I figured it out," said Hyacinth. "But only through big holes and hollows and cracks and doorways. Can it work with something tiny?"

The faerie chewed his lip silently.

"That's why we're using this room?" Caleb asked. "Because of that box? We could carry it anywhere."

"No." Hyacinth shook her head. "We won't touch it or disturb it. I don't want it disrupted any more than it will be. And it will be disrupted a lot." She focused on the faerie. "Well? Will you show me how?"

"Two pies," the faerie said. "Every Christmas."

Hyacinth smiled. "Deal."

"One meat," he added.

"No way," Hyacinth said. "Fruit only."

The faerie frowned, disappointed. Hyacinth burst out laughing.

"Of course meat," she said. "Whatever the outlaw is weird enough to want. Now show me."

A distant door banged shut. Voices. They all heard them and froze.

Hyacinth glanced at Mordecai. "I'd get to work on your vine thing. Fast."

NIMIANE WALKED QUICKLY THROUGH her garden, past the metal trees and over the false grass made of feathers. She twisted around and between her maze walls until she stood in front of a doorway of cold stone, unlike anything else around it. Nimiane paused, stroking Bast. She could summon slaves and a coach and another army. But there was no point. And there was reason to hurry. If the fools were able to free her father, it would require a great deal of pain and effort and possible destruction to return him to his cage.

She already had men in the field giving chase. And from the center of her garden labyrinth, old Endor and her mad ancestors were only one step away.

Nimiane hated the old city and its dust, its death, and its wandering mad. It stood as a monument to her father's failure. A monument to her own eventual failure ... her doom.

She stepped into the door and out into a moonlit square crowded with blade slaves and hunters and witch-dogs. A tower of ravens spun slowly in the moonlit air.

Nimiane looked for a commander. A tall blade with broad shoulders and a black pointed beard stood nearest, hands on his hips, assessing the structure of the tomb halls.

"Mordred," the witch said. "Where are they?"

The man spun around, surprised, and then bowed his head.

"Queen!"

On all sides, men turned and bowed.

"We tracked them here, Queen, although we were ambushed by faeren along the way. Hunters are searching the tomb halls now. Why they came here, I don't know."

"Because Nimroth is here," Nimiane said, and she walked up beside her warrior as Bast eyed the crumbling stone facade.

"I don't understand, Queen," Mordred said. "What would they want with him?"

"Imagine the Blackstar free," Nimiane said, "and understand. Send blades to his tomb immediately."

Even as she said it, a man carrying two curved swords emerged from the building in a hurry.

"Hunters back!" he yelled. "Witch-dogs front!" Seeing the queen, he ran through the crowd toward her, dropping to one knee and rising again when he arrived.

"We have them trapped, Queen," the man said. "But the green man has thrown up vines of fire we cannot cut. When the wizards—"

"The wizards will fail. In whose tomb is he trapped?"

"I do not know the tombs, Queen."

Nimiane moved past him toward the arched entrance. She stroked Bast's head as she went, and her soldiers and hunters parted around her.

HYACINTH SAT WITH HER back against the stone wall and watched Mordecai work. It was possible that she was going to wake up and find that none of this was happening, that she was actually sleeping in the trailer, wedged uncomfortably between her two sisters. Just the thought made her ache with desire. She wanted to smell her sisters. To laugh at them. To know them more deeply than she ever had.

She knew that was unlikely now.

Kibs sat beside her, also watching. Mordecai moved his body like a painter, like a conductor of music that only he could hear, brushing his palm over every stone in the walls, over every chink and every crack, ghosting green and gold and purple over the surface and deep into the stone.

Outside the room, the hall was full of shouting and snarling.

"Hunters back!" a voice bellowed.

"Aye, get back!" Caleb yelled. "Run!"

"Witch-dogs front!" the voice shouted, and then Caleb ducked quickly into the room as an arrow streaked past and a spear clattered onto the floor.

Caleb looked at his brother. "Ready?" he asked.

"Mmm," Mordecai answered. "Nearly."

"Could wizards get me through your net out there?" Caleb asked. "Because it's their turn to try."

"Yes," Mordecai said. "I threw that one up quickly. They'll get it down. This is the one that matters."

Hyacinth looked at the little box on the shelf for the hundredth time, and Kibs saw her look. And he saw Hyacinth's knee begin to bounce.

"It will work," Kibs said. "It will. We'll get through."

"Are you sure?" Hyacinth asked.

The faerie shrugged. "May as well be. If we all die, at least we can die without having to worry about it first. Just one fleeting moment of disappointment, and then poof."

Hyacinth let both of her knees begin to bounce.

A blast of fire and wind washed down the hall and into the room.

"Mordecai," Caleb said. "Now or never."

"Almost," Mordecai said. Sweat was dripping off of him when he finally moved to the door, his hand gliding continuously. "Just double-checking," he said. "If she's in here forever, I know she will. It all has to . . . connect . . . and feed. . . ."

Smoke filled the hallway and trickled in the doorway. A moment later, the stone floor shivered and a mass of vines flew past down the hall.

"Mordecai!" Caleb yelled, and two large wizards stepped into view.

Mordecai stood motionless, only two feet away from them. They looked at his glowing flat hand, and then at his face.

"Well," the first one said, "that was easy."

The second one grinned and reached across the threshold.

Mordecai closed his fist, and a portcullis of gold and green fire, dotted with purple, slammed shut, severing the man's arm at the elbow.

Screaming, the wizard hurled a curse at Mordecai. It didn't touch him, but the ghost vines woven through the stones glowed dimly.

Mordecai backed into the center of the room and watched, curious, as flames and wind and ice tore at his wall of vine fire. None of it managed to enter the room.

"It's working," Caleb said.

Mordecai nodded. He backed across the room and sat down beside Hyacinth. Caleb followed.

While all four of them sat and watched, wizards worked and wizards cursed, and the stones glowed strong on every side—in the ceiling, through the air, across the floor, and around a little box, sitting on a shelf.

"How much longer until they give up and she comes?" Caleb asked. "One day? Two? Should we try to sleep?"

Hyacinth laughed. "You're crazy," she said. "There's a severed arm on the floor and however many wizards are out there trying to kill us while we've locked ourselves into some kind of tomb. I could stay awake for a week in here."

"I brought cheese," Kibs offered. "But not much."

"Way!" a voice shouted. "Way for the witch-queen!"

The curses and fire and wind all stopped. The wizards, sweaty and panting, stepped back.

Mordecai and Caleb jumped to their feet. Hyacinth started to slide toward the box, but Kibs grabbed her.

Nimiane stepped into the doorway. Her face was beautiful but hard, and her hair gleamed in the light from Mordecai's fire vines. Her eyes were empty, but her hands were full. Bast, with his white fur patchy with scabs, looked at Hyacinth and hissed.

Nimiane stretched out her hand but stopped short of touching the flickering vine.

"Strange," she said. "To what end, green blood? You cannot stop me."

And the witch-queen hit the cage with all the strength she had. The light surged and then dimmed.

"Why this tomb?" she asked. "Why any of this? You could rise above all the witch-dogs in my armies."

"You're afraid," Mordecai said quietly. "You think that

I will die here? That I am trapped? I am not. I will do what I came here to do, and then I will walk away."

Nimiane lifted her blind face toward the ceiling, but the cat stared at Mordecai, unblinking, lashing its tail.

"And what, green blood, did you come here to do?"

Mordecai bent his knees, meeting eyes with the cat at her level.

"I cannot kill you," he said. "But I will see you thrown down." He straightened and took a step back. "Hyacinth, it's time to leave."

Hyacinth slid to her knees and crouched in front of the box.

"No!" Nimiane snarled, and her real attack came. She hit the cage with the force of lightning, and Hyacinth's ears screamed with the blow. Mordecai slipped and fell.

"Remember, the box isn't there," Kibs whispered in Hyacinth's ear. "Your eyes are liars. We've helped the grain find somewhere else. Something else. It's waiting already."

Hyacinth wondered where she was going. Another island? A faeren mound? Or maybe one of the trees in California beside the house she barely knew?

The vine fire flickered around her. She couldn't think about that. None of that mattered.

Hyacinth Smith shut her eyes, slid her fingers inside a small box, felt a pull as violent and constant as a waterfall, and dove forward.

The top of her head slammed into something painfully

hard. Something cracked, but not her skull. Panic flooded through her. She was stuck, half in and half out. Was the cupboard blocked on the other side? A tree? A rock?

Hyacinth splayed her bare toes on the stone floor and scrambled in place. A small chain was digging into her face. She splayed her toes again and tried to push, but her toes wouldn't grip.

Someone put two hands on her backside and shoved her forward so hard that her face skipped across a wood floor and banged into another wall. Rolling onto her back, she looked around. She had just emerged from the very bottom of a wall into a tiny attic room. The wall was made entirely of doors. So many doors. A small black one with a gold chain attached to the inside lay loose on the ground. Dry glue was crusted around its lip. Someone had tried to seal it shut. A bucket sat in the corner, but otherwise, the room was empty. The only light was yellow and incandescent and entering through the room's open doorway.

Kibs wriggled out of the wall facedown and then rolled away quickly.

"How's it going?" Hyacinth asked.

The faerie shook dust and ash from his hair. "Not good. That woman could drink the whole world. Where are we?"

"In someone's house, I think," Hyacinth said. "An attic, from the look of the ceiling."

Kibs nodded. "We should go."

"No." Hyacinth was surprised by the certainty in her voice. "We should wait."

"He'd want us—"

"I don't care."

NIMIANE FOUGHT TO DRAIN the fiery vines in front of her, straining at the cage that kept her from the sons of the eye-thief. Bast sat on her shoulder, looking down on her shorter enemy. Inside, so close she could taste his sweat, the boy fought to stop her, with arms spread and hands touching stone on both sides of the doorway.

"Go!" the boy yelled at his brother. "Go! I can't hold her."

The other boy shook his head.

"Now!" Mordecai screamed.

Reluctantly, his brother obeyed, dropping to his knees and worming his way into nothingness.

It didn't matter. When the cage was down, Nimiane could drain them all dry through an opening half that size.

Gathering the full force of her devouring hunger, Nimiane pulled at the cage. There was so much power in it, so much life, and in a moment all of it would be inside her, feeding her.

The boy's hands slipped off the walls, and he staggered backward. The cage across the open doorway opened as he did.

Nimiane laughed. Happiness was not something she

often felt—the primitive happiness of a child inflicting pain and taking what she wants.

Mordecai was panting, sweating, but for some reason, he didn't look scared. His hand was open, fingers spread, palm on fire, ready to fight on.

Nimiane didn't think about how the cage had opened. It had not been absorbed, and she did not even notice. She didn't fear anything that this powerful little green blood could do to her. And why should she? He wasn't his father.

Still laughing, ready to devour, she stepped across the threshold.

Bast tensed. And the boy smiled.

"You think that was a fight?" Mordecai asked. He clenched his fist, and the cage of fire dropped back down behind her. He jerked his arm and the iron door slammed shut on the outside, with its own web of vines glowing, inside and out.

Nimiane spun in surprise, confusion not yet fully turned to fear.

"Green blood," she said. "You think this can hold me?"

The boy dropped to his knees and dove at the swirl of nothingness that had swallowed his brother.

Nimiane leapt for his legs, closing both claw hands tightly around his ankles. There was so much strength still in him that it burned her as it flooded in. And then she felt the heat of his palm press against her face. The blow from that touch spun her across the room and slammed her into the wall with a tangle of fiery rope around her throat and face.

HYACINTH AND CALEB DRAGGED Mordecai into the attic room. Caleb grabbed the black cupboard lid and slammed it back in place. Mordecai spun around on his belly, shut his eyes, and pressed his palm against the door, tracing the outline.

Then he let his face fall to the floor. He was pale and breathing hard, pooling sweat.

But his eyes were open and they met Hyacinth's. He smiled.

"We did it," he said.

"Let's see if it holds," said Caleb.

"It will hold," Mordecai said. "Unless one of our family opens it."

"That looks uncomfortable," Hyacinth said. "Here, sit up."

"No," Mordecai said. "Not moving for a year. This feels fantastic." And he shut his eyes.

NIMIANE PACED IN THE DARKNESS. The boy had closed and sealed the way behind him, linking it up to the whole cage. But she could still feel lives in the hallway outside. She could hear voices calling for her.

Again, she threw her strength at the web, and again

the room merely brightened. Already she was exhausted. Empty. A blind and scabby hag.

How was this possible?

It wasn't. She could wield more life than a nation. She reached out through the iron door and found lives, lives she needed. She took them quickly, to the last drop, until their souls were gone and their bodies ash. Life after life after life she gathered, until the men outside no longer screamed and she felt them fleeing. But too slowly.

Nimiane, witch-queen of Endor, daughter of Nimroth, raged. For hours she raged, hurling every life she could gather at the green blood's vines until they burned so bright and hot that the stone melted around them. Her skin blistered, and Bast writhed in pain on the floor. All night she raged, until she no longer had enough strength to burn the stones. Until there were no more lives within her reach. Until she had turned her army into ash and herself into a shivering crone, bleeding black undying blood on the floor of her forever.

And then, for the first time in three and a half centuries, Nimiane of Endor wept.

Outside, as the moon set on old Endor, on abandoned weapons and empty clothes and muttering madmen, a cool breeze climbed down from the sky and redusted the streets with the ashes of the queen's army.

BENEATH ANOTHER MOON, IN a place called Kansas, three companions and a faerie talking about pie limped down a narrow country road toward a small country town. A three-story farmhouse with a glowing attic window stood behind them. Wind chimes called to them from the porch, but they didn't listen.

One of them stood straight, and his smile was quick. One was bent in pain but happy. And one of them was a girl with bruised bare feet, who felt lighter than light itself. And one of them was a faerie, grinning and pulling his wiry hair down around his ears (and talking about pie).

All of them were hungry. Starving. But they were in search of a city park, where the faerie promised there was a tree with a wide hole that he knew from long ago.

"Where are we?" Mordecai asked.

"Does it matter?" Kibs answered.

No. No, it didn't matter. Not to them. Not right then. But while they walked, Hyacinth looked up at a high-legged silver water tower, standing guard over the entire town. Painted in large block letters on the tower's belly, there was a simple name.

HENRY

And suddenly she missed her family desperately and wanted to throw her arms around her mother and kiss her father and laugh with her sisters and listen to her brothers taunt each other despite the years between them.

"Are you okay?" Mordecai asked.

"I think so," Hyacinth said. "At least, I'm pretty sure I will be. You?"

"Yeah," Mordecai said, rolling his shoulder. "Pretty sure I will be."

FOURTEEN

LAWRENCE AND HARRIET AND Circe and Daniel all sat on the end of a long dock, with their legs in frigid water. Across the lake, steep tree-lined mountains rose up from the water. Behind them, there was laughter and splashing and a camp bustling with kids of almost every age.

"I don't understand," Lawrence said. "What rules did she break? She said it wasn't magic. I was there."

Circe slid her arm around her little brother's shoulders. "Sounds pretty magical to me," she said. "And amazing."

"Super amazing," Lawrence said. "Hy was the awesomest. Stupid rules."

"Well, yeah," said Daniel. "Aren't they usually?"

Harriet sniffed and wiped her eyes. "At least Mom and Dad found her. And she's with a nice family. I hope they aren't the only ones who get to visit. They have to let us visit."

"I'll make them," Lawrence said. "I don't care about the rules."

"Hush," Circe said. "In public, we talk like she's dead. Like she never happened. Always."

"It's just us, C," Daniel said. "I won't pretend when it's just us."

"It isn't," Circe whispered. "Look." And she nodded toward the shore.

All four heads turned and focused on a kid standing on the dock. He was Lawrence's age and build, but with black skin, a squarer jaw, and a more serious face. At the moment, he was wearing tight gray shorts and knee socks with stripes, along with a blue shirt with his family crest centered in silver on the chest—a chess knight with wings.

"Rupert Greeves," Circe said. "Welcome to the dock."

"Hey, Rupe," Lawrence said.

"Hey," Rupert said. "If you like, I'll show you the obstacle course. I hold the course record for the under-twelves."

"Oh, do you?" Daniel laughed. "L, I think that's a challenge."

"Or," Rupert said, "if you prefer a swim, I'll race you to the buoys."

"And do you hold the swim record as well?" Circe asked.

"For the under-twelves," Rupert said, "I do."

Lawrence pulled his feet out of the water and stood, crossing his arms to face Rupert.

"Which record is your favorite?" he asked.

Rupert shook his head. "What?"

"I'll let you keep one," Lawrence said. "And you get to pick which one."

Daniel whooped, and even Harriet smiled.

Rupert's eyes narrowed. "They are all my favorite," he said.

"Fine," Lawrence said. "I'll decide which one you get to keep. Take me to the obstacle course."

Harriet and Circe and Daniel watched the two boys jog away.

"Well," Circe said, "they're going to hate each other."

Daniel shook his head. "No, I don't think so. I think L just replaced me. New best friend for life."

MANY MILES SOUTH, ABOVE a cliff beside the sea, Trudie and Albert Smith stood beside young Robert Boone and watched crews with saws milling the Grove of Ways into timber.

One hundred yards away, Thor was overseeing the crackling blaze. Already, every frame in the barn and house had been consumed.

As for Granlea's body, Trudie had refused to have her buried anywhere near the property. The Order had taken her away, and as the nearest kin, they had asked the Smiths for an epitaph.

Albert had resisted the temptation to etch SHE GOT WHAT SHE WANTED onto the tombstone, but since everything positive had seemed disingenuous, they kept it limited to her name.

Robert Boone had asked if they would like Hyacinth to be remembered with a stone as well. Albert and Trudie had told him absolutely not. She was alive, they were sure of it, living in another world—except, they insisted, there really is only one world, but it's a tangle of branches and grains and rings and times. Hyacinth was out there. And someday, they assured Robert Boone, they would find her, and she would be vindicated.

Sometimes, they knew, the best way to deceive is to tell the truth.

Meanwhile, beside a different sea, beneath a different sun, in a different branch of this one world, Hyacinth stood on a rooftop.

She was laughing.

How could she not be when the cathedral bells were ringing in every town along that stormy fishing coast? When the city gates had been thrown open and horses were prancing, throwing sparks from their shoes, and the people of the city, and in every city along that coast, were roasting fish and chestnuts in the streets, and there was dancing and music in every square, and Caleb and Mordecai had been paraded around for days, and they were sick of it, and she had refused to have any part of it—other than dancing and laughing and eating too much?

She had found her parents in time, before the Grove

of Ways was burned, and she brought them to this town. They saw where she would live and met Mordecai's mother and watched her remove Mordecai's fungal bite and were amazed.

Although her parents' eyes had been wet when they'd left—and so had hers—she knew, as long as the trees wrapped time and memory inside their rings, there would be a doorway home.

She only had to find it.

Beside her on that rooftop, with his wings spread and his nose raised, her charcoal raggant felt the same.

GRATITUDE

Rory, Lucia, Ameera, Seamus, and Marisol for Listening
Heather Linn for Prodding
Chelsea E for Green Pencil Faces
Team RHCB for Not Quitting
The O of B for Still Kicking
Cyrus and Antigone for Hanging In There

About the Author

N. D. WILSON lives and writes in the top of a tall, skinny house only one block from where he was born. But his bestselling novels, including the highly acclaimed 100 Cupboards series, have traveled far and wide and been translated into dozens of languages. He and his wife have five young storytellers of their own, along with an unreasonable number of pets. You can visit him online at ndwilson.com.